ALOE AND GOODBYE

RUBY SHAW MYSTERIES, BOOK ONE

JANICE PEACOCK

Vetrai Press

ALSO BY JANICE PEACOCK

For Mom,
a gardener
extraordinaire

ONE

My name is Ruby Shaw. At least it is today.

It was something else two weeks ago, but I'm not allowed to use my real name anymore. That was what Victor Wilson, the US marshal who'd dumped us off in this godforsaken little town in Arizona, told me. And my daughter? Yes, she had to choose a new name too. She picked Allison—Allie for short—which wasn't too different from her birth name.

Standing shoulder to shoulder at the bottom of the stairs, we watched as Victor drove away in his plain black sedan, down the long, steep street and around one of the numerous switchbacks that riddled this hillside town. Above us, the hills were illuminated by a brilliant sunset—bursts of purples and oranges I wished I could capture on a painted canvas.

With our witness protection officer out of sight, Allie and I turned wordlessly and climbed the concrete steps to our new home. It had been painted haphazardly in the steps' color, a dismal gray, more or less matching my mood.

Allie's new black backpack and my blue duffel held our meager belongings, which we carried up the steps. Victor had allowed us to do some shopping at the Kmart some twenty miles away in Wendlewood. Everything we purchased was plain —nothing artful or unique. "Fly under the radar," Victor had said. Our lives depended on it.

The hinges squeaked in protest as I opened the front door. Holding my breath, I took Allie's hand, and we stepped inside the house. What was supposed to be the living room held a bedraggled sofa and not much more. It hadn't changed much since Victor had shown it to us a few days before. He had promised me we'd have a fully furnished house by now. Where the heck was everything? I put on a brave face for Allie, but inside I was cussing out Victor and his flunkies.

But looking around gave me hope. The living room had large windows spanning the front wall and straight ahead was a cozy kitchen. Maybe this wasn't going to be too horrible after we had some furniture and settled in.

Allie didn't share my optimism. She turned away and stealthily wiped a tear. At twelve, she didn't like anyone, including her mother, seeing her cry.

"Sweetheart, it's not going to be so bad," I said as I turned her toward me and hugged her tight. Over her shoulder, I watched as an enormous mouse scurried out the open front door. At least he was headed *out* and not *in*. I released my child and closed the door—no sense in having the mouse change its mind and come back inside.

Allie didn't look convinced. She sniffled and wiped her nose on her black sweatshirt. Today wasn't a day to scold her for that. She looked so small in her oversize hoodie, but had recently started growing and would soon pass me at five foot five. Puberty was going to be another harrowing adventure for us, no doubt.

"You're going to be okay. We both are. You and I are made of strong stuff, remember that." Allie nodded as she looked down at her pristine black Converse sneakers. "Let's take a look around." We made our way down a short hallway that ended in a bathroom and a bedroom on each side.

"Which room do you want?" I asked. Allie pointed to the left. "Good choice, you'll get the morning sun," I said as cheerfully as possible as I followed her in, turning on the overhead light as we entered. The room smelled stale, like it had been closed up for too long, and it was utterly empty except for a twin bed with a pile of linens, still in their packages, on top of the mattress. "You've got a bed. Isn't that wonderful?" Allie rolled her eyes. Okay, maybe I was piling the cheerfulness on a little thick.

"Don't worry, I'll make sure Victor gets you a desk and chair. I promise," I said as I closed the shabby drapes on the window next to her bed. "And tomorrow we'll get this place opened up to get some fresh air in here."

I had to admit my positive attitude was starting to wane. Allie was taking this pretty hard, and I knew I needed to be enthusiastic for both of us, though I wondered how long I'd be able to keep it up.

"Okay, baby, let's get your bed set up."

I slid the sheets out of the packaging as I looked around the room, imagining how we could turn this into a terrific place for a tween. It was a challenge figuring out what Allie liked these days. Mostly, her clothes were all black, and so was her attitude. Gone was the delightful and curious child who used to run through Central Park, ready and willing to pet any dog that crossed her path or make friends with any child on the playground.

"I don't want to take the time to wash the sheets. I'm not even sure if we have a washing machine, but I will take care of everything tomorrow," I said as I struggled to pull the fitted sheet onto the mattress. Allie glowered at me. She'd been doing that a lot lately. While I finished making the bed, Allie found her pj's and put them on. She pulled out an iPod from her backpack and put the earbuds in her ears. This was a sure sign that she wanted some space.

I found a similar setup to Allie's in my bedroom: a bed and a dresser. Whoever had purchased these things for us had been thoughtful enough to choose a queen bed for me. After making up my bed and unpacking my bag, I surveyed the rest of the house. We had a cute little bathroom with mint-green tile. It needed an update, but as long as I thought of it as vintage instead of old, it suited us just fine. I was relieved to see we had TP and towels, but there was so much more we needed. I examined my face in the bathroom mirror. The dark circles beneath my eyes reminded me that the events of the last few weeks, and especially that terrible night in Las Vegas, had taken their toll on me.

How could this have happened to us? It wasn't a productive question tonight or any other night for that matter.

Returning to Allie's room, I found her dozing off. I brushed her light brown hair from her forehead. As I gently pulled the earbuds from her ears, I kissed her good night.

"Night night, sweetheart," I said as I shut off the light.

"Mom? Can you leave the hall light on?" She'd left everything and everyone she knew behind, and she was hurting because of it. At least the light would bring her a little comfort.

"Of course," I said, doing just that.

I wandered into the kitchen and idly opened the cupboards. We'd had dinner in Wendlewood, so I wasn't hungry but did wonder if they—whoever *they* were—had thought to stock the kitchen with food. They hadn't. It appeared they hadn't done much of anything to prepare for our arrival. I found a single bottle of Budweiser in the back of a cupboard, but no opener. Catching the edge of the cap on the side of the counter, I whacked the top of the bottle. It worked like a charm, just as I remembered back in art school. Miraculously, there was ice in the freezer, along with a can of orange juice concentrate. If I had some vodka, I could have made a screwdriver instead of drinking a beer, but no such luck.

I found an empty jelly jar in one of the cupboards, which I rinsed out and filled with ice. Then I poured the beer into my makeshift glass. Beer on ice might be unconventional, but it beat warm beer any day of the week. I pulled my new cell phone, courtesy of the US government, out of my jeans' back pocket, and called Victor. He would be our lifeline while we were in the Witness Protection Program, WITSEC for short.

Victor had done what he could to protect us and had repeated the rules of the program until we'd memorized them: We weren't to get in touch with our family, friends, or anyone else from our past. We weren't allowed to bring our old belongings, including photos, art, or anything else that might identify us. Victor had gone easy on us, allowing each of us a special item. For Allie, it was her iPod, and for me, it was my mother's ruby ring. We had to assume new identities, including changing our names and, in my case, giving up a career I loved. All of our belongings were now in storage, and if we were ever safe enough to leave the WITSEC program, we'd get those things—and our lives—back.

Since Victor didn't answer his phone, I left him a message. He was likely still on the road after dropping us off.

"Hi, Victor. It's, uh, Ruby," I said. I wondered how long it would be before I felt comfortable referring to myself by my new name. "I need you to call me back. We need help. All we have are beds and a sofa. How about an armchair, a couple of lamps, a coffee table? Oh, and Allie needs a desk. Call me." It was Sunday night, and I doubted I'd hear anything from him until tomorrow.

I opened the back door and stood on the small landing, looking down at the side yard, which sloped precipitously to an overgrown gulch below. Our house clung to the hillside, like everything else in this town. I took the steep, rickety staircase to a terraced yard behind the house. Tucked up next to the house, there was a wooden porch with a narrow, shingled roof and a wide railing running along the front edge. At the end of the porch was a storage shed, its door hanging open with not much more than cobwebs inside.

As I looked at the barren earth beneath my feet, something stirred inside me. Someone had taken the time to terrace the yard, but had they ever grown anything? What could I do with this land? It seemed to me that if a person planted something, and if they watched it grow, it meant they intended to stick around. And I intended to stay in this place. I recalled what my father had told me: Start with the earth. He had been a successful farmer, and I knew he was right. In all endeavors, start from the ground and work up.

The sound of coyotes yipping in the distance echoed up from the canyon with a cool evening breeze. It had been a long time since I'd heard that high-pitched keening, and it added to my anxiety. In recent years, the only wildlife I'd encountered were well-fed rats in back alleys and clubbers after they'd left bars at two in the morning.

I mounted the stairs back up to the landing by the kitchen door and looked toward the dimly lit street. As I stood quietly in the dark, a group of people gathered in front of the house next door, just a few yards from where Victor had dropped us off.

A man was speaking to the gathering, but I was too far away to hear him. Those who had flashlights aimed their beams at the house and their guide. I could see that their leader was a tall, thin man wearing a bowler hat and long black coat through the shadowy light. The group ascended the front steps and entered my neighbor's house. How very odd.

After a few minutes, screams pierced the quiet darkness, and the group pushed its way out the front door, running as if fleeing for their lives—steps behind them, an ax-wielding hooded figure chased after the group.

Holy crap! I dropped my beer off the side of the railing, stumbling backward in shock. What was I supposed to do? Call 911? Victor had told me to try and blend in—calling 911 on our first night in town was definitely not flying under the radar. My heart pounding, I yanked my phone from my back pocket to call Victor. I doubted he'd answer since he hadn't picked up just moments ago.

Frozen in place, I watched in horror from my vantage point as the scene next door unfolded. But no one was screaming in terror now. No one was covered in blood. The cloaked figure with the ax went back inside the house while the group members laughed and clutched each other as the leader of their group—presumably a tour guide—ushered everyone up the towering hill beyond my home, toward the center of town.

There was no need to call Victor or 911. What the heck had just happened?

It had to have been some sort of spooky tour. Victor had mentioned that Paradise was a former ghost town. This little show must have been someone's way of capitalizing on that fact. I had a friend in New York—a struggling actor, of course—who was a tour guide for the city's Vampire and Ghost Tour. He told me all the ghost stories and theatrics were entirely fabricated, but apparently the tours brought in good money, and the tourists loved every scary moment.

Still rattled from what I'd seen, but glad that it was just a show, I went back inside, locked the kitchen door, and checked the lock on the front door as well.

Too amped up with adrenaline to sleep, I sat on the sofa in the living room, taking deep breaths to calm myself. I didn't even have my beer to drink, and tomorrow I'd have to go and find the broken jelly jar I'd dropped into the yard.

I sat for a long time making a mental list of what we'd need to restart our lives. I was a long way from the life I'd known in New York City. What little I'd seen of the town of Paradise was from the passenger seat of Victor's car. It all seemed sad and desolate. Or maybe I was just projecting.

According to Victor, Paradise, Arizona, had been built in 1890, when two prospectors—Rufus Parr and Willard Dice—discovered copper. Before a mine could open, there needed to be housing for the miners, and the only available land for miles around was a steep, rocky hillside. It was certainly not the most hospitable location to build a community. And the name Paradise? It was a combination of the two men's names, and then tweaked a little bit; Parr and Dice became Paradise. Calling the town Paradise seemed like wishful thinking. It wasn't the first name that came to mind as Victor drove through switchback after switchback with nothing to see but sagebrush and cacti at the side of the road.

Like it or not, Paradise was going to be home for Allie and me, for now, and maybe forever. Frankly, leading a simple life sounded good. It was a chance for us to try again. I'd made some choices that had been less than perfect, or more specifically, my sister had. The past was behind us now. There was no turning back.

TWO

The following morning, I woke up to the sound of a siren wailing nearby. This wasn't a good sign. I was curled up on the sofa in the living room, evidently having fallen asleep there and never making it to my bed.

I felt a twinge in my neck as I peered through the mini blinds. Sleeping on a lumpy couch wasn't good for my forty-something-year-old body. I managed to pull my long hair, which overnight had become a curly mess, into a ponytail.

A single SUV, the word *Sheriff* painted on its side panels, pulled into the driveway of my neighbor's house. Was this Paradise's entire law enforcement team? I wouldn't doubt it. Whatever was happening, I wanted to stay far, far away from it. I dreaded being interrogated by a cop who would ask questions about why we were here—and who we were, for that matter. As I watched, another car pulled up to the curb, and a slender man trotted up the stairs. A woman in a tan uniform, likely a deputy, met him as he reached the porch. The man was agitated, and as I studied him, I realized he resembled the leader of last night's tour—assuming that was what I'd witnessed. Of course, other men fit that description, and since it was dark, I couldn't be sure what I'd seen last night.

I called Victor, and he answered.

"What can I do for you?" Victor's voice twanged in a slow Texan drawl, which somehow comforted me.

"I think something's happened next door, and I don't want you to think I had anything to do with it."

"Did you have anything to do with it?"

"No!" Then I thought about it. "Okay, so, I think I might have seen something—but maybe not. There was some sort of scary tour on my street. A guy with an ax chased a few people out the front door of my neighbor's house. I didn't think it was real, though."

"And now you're telling me that it was real? You just stay away from whatever is going on out there. Okay?"

"Okay, I promise. It's probably nothing. I mean, how high could the homicide rate be in a little town like this?"

"You'd be surprised. Anything else?"

"I need to talk with you about this house."

"What about it?"

"It's pretty dismal. We need some things to make this place a little cozier. We've got a couch, and that's it, in the living room. We could use an upholstered chair, a few lamps. Oh, and Allie needs a desk."

"I'm working on it."

"Can I buy some art supplies? Allie and I could paint something…."

"No painting for you. You're not an artist anymore. You don't want someone to recognize you by your work."

Victor was right. I'd been lucky to have become a successful artist. My distinctive, bold painting style had made me a darling in the New York galleries, as well as high-end specialty shops across the nation. There'd been articles in magazines about me, and I'd completed several high-profile commissions. But I couldn't create my art anymore, or I risked being recognized. Since I'd been in the public eye, they'd insisted I change my look.

The marshals were not happy with the multicolored streaks in my hair and suggested I dye it all one color. I'd have chosen a vibrant red for my long curly locks, to match my new name, but Victor frowned at that idea. My new hair color was dark brown, as it had been when I was younger. It was boring, but if it kept me safe, I'd learn to live with it.

"I know. It's just so plain around here. Maybe I could buy a few things to make this house less sterile. I've told you about my beautiful art-filled apartment next to Central Park, right? You know what it was like before ... here."

"I know, I know. I will personally make sure you get the furniture you need. We'll set things right for you, but you need a little patience. You're going to need to give up that New Yorker pace if you know what's good for you."

"Got it. Loud and clear. Couldn't I just use some of the money in my bank account? Or Claudia's?"

"All of your sister's assets are frozen. Your assets are too, but I'm working on making some money transfers to fix that. It takes a little time."

"How much is 'a little'?"

"As long as it takes," he said, that slow drawl replaced by a terseness that told me he was losing his patience.

"If you'd just let me call my sister, I'm sure we could figure something out," I said, my intensity rising.

"Sorry. No. Not at this point. It's for your safety."

"But maybe someday? No need to even answer. I know what you're going to say, 'Be patient, Ruby.' So, where can I get some cash? We need some groceries, and maybe a little more clothing than what we bought in Wendlewood."

"We'll support you. You know that. But you also need to start thinking about a job."

I sighed. A job—a real nine-to-five job. I hadn't had one of those in years.

"You're going to have to be patient, these things take time," I said, throwing his advice right back at him. "So, how am I supposed to find this job? And how am I supposed to get there without a car?"

"I'm sure you know how to find a job. And as for transportation, you haven't yet shown a need for a car. If you find a job that requires one, you'll get one. In the meantime, we put you in a walkable location."

"If I were a mountain goat." I looked out the front window at the steep street that headed toward downtown Paradise.

"Think of it as good exercise. There's money, a checkbook, and an ATM card in the orange juice can in the freezer."

"Freezer?" I would've found it if I'd had vodka to make a screwdriver. A screwdriver sounded fantastic right now, but I reminded myself that day drinking wasn't a habit I'd ever indulged in.

"It's one place that crooks never look when they're robbing your house. I always like to think of it as cold, hard cash," Victor chuckled and hung up the phone.

I found a packet of chilly twenties inside the OJ can along with an ATM card and a checkbook, just as Victor promised. Thank heavens! At least Allie and I could get some food and a few other things to make it feel like home around here. I slipped out onto my back porch and watched as the medical examiner's truck drove away. A deputy was talking with the man who'd arrived a few minutes ago. Since I was too far away to hear what they were saying, I went inside and changed into a clean T-shirt and jeans. This would be my new uniform for living in small-town America, along with my completely unstylish white Keds. I found Allie sitting on the side of her bed, still in her pajamas.

"Good morning. How about some breakfast? Maybe we can find a café in town? Then we can go and find your new school."

Allie nodded as she got up from her bed and headed for her backpack to find an outfit for the day. She got dressed in another flavor of a black T-shirt, with black jeans, and her black sneakers.

"Let's see if we can find a shop and get you some more clothes too. That Kmart stuff wasn't the best. And somehow, you ended up with everything in black."

"On purpose," Allie mumbled as we headed for the door.

We hiked toward downtown, although it was more like *uptown* given the sharp incline of the street that led into Paradise proper, my thighs burning with each step. At least I'd be getting some good cardio since I didn't have a gym around the corner like in my old neighborhood. Arriving at a switchback, we turned the sharp corner and headed farther up the street. In the crook of another switchback at the edge of town, we spotted Bette's Place and went inside.

Inside the cozy café, booths ran along a row of windows and barstools were pushed up against an old-school Formica counter with the kitchen's order pickup window beyond it. In a standard-issue white uniform dress with a yellow apron, a waitress met us with menus as we entered. Her complexion was the color of copper, with a constellation of freckles across her nose and cheeks.

"Well now, who have we here? You folks visiting? Where are you from?" The woman peppered us with questions, leaving no time to answer. "My name's Bettenaya, but I go by Bette. Bettenaya? I know, such a long silly name! My mother must've been crazy to name me that. Not *must've*—she was *definitely* crazy," she said with a cackle, tossing back dozens of tiny braids on her head.

Bette, who looked to be about my age, kept up with questions as she took us to a booth. She didn't really wait for an answer, and the rest of the diner was busy and noisy. It felt good to be here, after weeks when our only contacts had been law enforcement.

"Coffee?" Bette asked. For the first time since we walked in, she waited for a response.

"Yes, I'll have a cappuccino—"

Bette held up two carafes of coffee, one in each hand.

"Decaf or caf?" she asked, giving me a patient, toothy grin. Ah. This wasn't a place where I could order any sort of espresso drink. Got it.

"I definitely want the caffeinated kind, please. And what do you want?" I asked Allie. She shrugged. "Chocolate milk for my mostly mute daughter."

Allie stared at me from across the table, but at least it wasn't a glare. Things had always been good between us, and this new attitude was uncharted territory for me. I knew that while things were rough for me, they were more challenging for Allie, and any small thing I could do to make her feel better would help with her adjustment. At least I hoped so.

We ordered pancakes and sat and listened to the buzz around us. Everyone seemed to be talking about the same thing: A woman was found dead in her home this morning.

Bette came back with our drinks. My curiosity was piqued, so I decided to see if I could get answers and not just questions from her.

"Excuse me, Bette? Could you tell me what happened? Did someone die?"

"Oh yes, Greta Stramtussle, the poor thing. Died in her house. She did so much for our little town. None of us would be here if it weren't for her! She was perfectly healthy, you know, getting up there in years, but aren't we all? The sheriff's department isn't saying what happened. I bet her heart just gave up on her. She was no spring chicken, ya know," Bette said, patting her chest where her heart-shaped name tag was pinned.

I would take Victor's advice and keep clear of anything that had to do with anyone's mysterious death. We had better—and frankly, more important—things to do like settling into our new home and getting Allie started at school.

"I'm so sorry. I'm sure Mrs. Stramtussle's family and friends are upset."

"You never said—you're not from around here, are you? Just passing through?"

"We just moved in. We're living on Castlerock Road, just down the hill from here."

"Castlerock Road? Are you living in that old house there, number thirty-three?"

"As a matter of fact, we are."

"Oh! Well, then you live right next door to the house where Mrs. Stramtussle died. May she rest in peace."

I hoped that the woman had simply died of natural causes. If she hadn't, I'd likely have a cop knocking on my door later today, which made me shudder. I wasn't sure I was ready to recite my newly created background, especially not to someone trained to interrogate people.

Allie and I finished our breakfast and went off to explore the rest of downtown. Just past an animal rescue storefront, we found a small clothing shop and stopped in. Allie made a beeline for a rack of T-shirts, while I looked at some handmade felt purses in all the colors of the rainbow. I wanted to buy one, to give myself a present for having made it this far, but Victor's scolding about not standing out echoed through me. I looked down at my plain brown purse. It would have to do for now.

Allie found a black T-shirt with a green cactus on it. Underneath the image, it read, Handle with Care. While I always encouraged her to show her creativity and her true self through her clothing, this new desire of hers to dress in all black like Johnny Cash was something I'd not expected.

At least the shirt she chose had a fun image on it. As recently as a few months ago, she would have spent hours choosing hair ribbons and selecting the perfect sundress, but that was behind us, at least for the time being. As I looked around, it occurred to me that working in a shop like this could be fun. I took Allie's shirt to the register. A squat woman with a long braid of vibrant red hair sat behind the counter, knitting a colorful rectangle that was likely destined to become another felted purse.

"Great shop you have here," I said as I placed Allie's new shirt on the counter by the cash register.

"Thanks," the woman said, as she continued working on her knitting project.

"We just moved here," I said, trying to chat her up in hopes I could casually ask about any job openings.

"Hm. Well, that's nice," the woman said, finally looking up and checking the tag on the shirt for a price.

"We'll come back and buy a few more things soon."

"Sadly, it's our last week in business." This woman's voice was almost entirely devoid of emotion. It made me wonder whether she was like this with everyone or particularly indifferent to me. "We're going to switch over to being an online-only store after that."

Rats! So much for an employment opportunity.

"I'm sorry to hear that. You've got such cute things, and all handmade, too."

"We're just not getting enough foot traffic up here. They promised me so much when we rented this spot. They said the tourists would be pouring in. Well, that hasn't happened." Her tone sounded more pessimistic by the minute.

"If you hear of anyone needing help, I'm looking for a job. I'm Ruby." I offered her my hand for a friendly shake. She shook my hand but didn't provide her name.

"And you are?"

"Sorry, I'm just a little preoccupied. I'm Sally Graber. Nice to meet you," she said, as she wrapped the shirt and put it in a handled shopping bag for us. It was a splurge, and I was feeling a bit guilty about it. The shirt seemed to cheer up Allie the tiniest bit, and that was a move in the right direction. Victor wasn't going to give me money forever, and I had to get a job—sooner rather than later.

As we walked, I remembered all the times Allie and I went shopping together in New York. We loved to visit Macy's, especially at Christmas, to see the sparkling lights and festive decorations. As I thought ahead to the holidays, I wondered what they would be like for us this year. When my parents were still alive, we'd visit them and have a family Christmas. Before she passed away, my mother always made tamales, just like my grandmother used to make. My father insisted on making posole—a soup made with hominy—which was always so spicy we couldn't eat more than a bowl without breaking into a sweat. At times my sister, Claudia, and her husband, Ricky, would show up. They would arrive at the last minute and never stayed for long.

As we walked, I thought about Claudia and wondered where she was now. I had been whisked away by the marshals after I saw Claudia's husband kill a man at a hotel late one night. Ricky was arrested for his involvement with the Mexican Mafia's drug trade, and I ended up in witness protection so I could testify against him. Allie arrived the next day at the hotel where the marshals had housed me temporarily. With my permission, she was escorted by a marshal who had picked her up in New York and brought her to me.

The marshals never told me what happened to Claudia. I was unsure if she was also in witness protection and wondered how much she knew about her husband's dirty business dealings. I hoped she was in WITSEC and that I'd see her again someday.

THREE

Allie and I strolled along Stewart Street, a shop-filled road which had a hairpin turn at one end and a staircase in the middle that connected the upper and lower blocks. Each of the quaint stores had a tiny metal sign above its door indicating what the building had been back when the town was first built —a blacksmith, a saloon, a bank, a general store. Each had its original façade or had been rebuilt to look like a storefront from the late 1800s. The side of a building at the end of the street was painted with an ancient Levi's advertisement, now peeling to reveal the worn red brick wall. I still had my reservations about living out in the desert but was intrigued by this funky little town.

We arrived at the next switchback and turned the corner. Up ahead was Paradise School, an unassuming low-slung cinder block building. It was quite utilitarian, and about the same color as my house, no doubt a Pantone color called Drab Gray. We arrived during recess and watched children, who were much younger than Allie, as they played handball against a concrete wall with fat, red balls. Other children sat at metal tables on a scruffy patch of grass chatting and eating snacks.

What struck me was how different this school was from the private school Allie used to attend. At the Hawthorne Academy, ivy-covered brick walls encircled the campus. Every child wore a navy jacket and white shirt, part of the required school uniform, which, along with a tuition payment rivaling an Ivy League school, was merely what you did if you wanted your child to get an excellent education in the Big Apple.

Allie's father, who had decided early on in Allie's life that he wasn't cut out for parenthood, had left her some money he hoped would make up for the fact that he wouldn't be around to raise her. While that endowment had meant we had no problem paying Allie's tuition, she didn't have a father in her life, nor did I have a partner to help me raise my child. It was just Allie and me, which was fine with me. As for Allie, she couldn't miss someone she had never known and had turned out to be a pretty well-adjusted girl.

While this new school was different from what she had experienced thus far, it reminded me of what school had been like for Claudia and me when we were young—no uniforms, no tuition, and no nannies dropping off well-groomed students each morning. Instead, we rode our bikes a mile down the road to Clovis Elementary School in California's Central Valley.

"Come on, let's go find the principal," I said, heading up the steps to the administrative offices while Allie grudgingly followed three steps behind. We found the office and took a tentative step inside. A harried woman in her mid-thirties with a strawberry-blond pixie cut cradled a phone in the crook of her neck and took a message on a notepad while trying to put a thermometer in the mouth of a boy standing behind her desk. If this woman had an extra hand, I imagined she could be typing an e-mail and stuffing envelopes simultaneously. She finished with her message, hung up the phone, and clamped the boy's mouth around the thermometer all at once, a smooth move of multitasking if ever I'd seen one.

"How can I help you today?" the secretary asked, stuffing a note in the principal's inbox and tossing some paperclips into a kid-made clay bowl before turning her full attention to Allie and me. I didn't think she knew how to do one thing at a time.

"I'm Ruby Shaw, and this is Allie. We're new here, and I need to get her set up to attend seventh grade. She's anxious to start right away." Allie stood next to me and silently nodded her head.

"Nice to meet you. I'm Meg," she said, her hand lightly touching mine in the quickest of handshakes. "Now, let me see. Okay, it looks like we've got your daughter enrolled. I'm sure the principal wants to meet you," she said as she flipped over a pile of folders on her desk, grabbed one, and headed down the hall at a near trot. While Meg went to check with the principal, I noticed the name plaque on the desk. Ms. Stramtussle. Rats! Meg was another Stramtussle. She had to be related to the recently deceased Greta Stramtussle. Judging from Meg's age, she was likely Greta's daughter.

"Okay, the principal is ready for you," Meg said, popping around the corner to get us. We followed her down a short hall to a cramped office stuffed with books where the principal stood in the doorway.

"Please come in. Sit, sit!" She sidled past us and into the hall. "Meg? Have you seen my red glasses? I can't seem to find them anywhere."

"Sorry, ma'am, no," Meg said. "If you don't mind, I'm going to leave now. I need to talk with my brother about ... you know."

"Of course, dear. Take as much time as you need," Mrs. Heard said. She turned to us and added "Meg found out early this morning that her mother has passed away. I told her not to come in to work, but she wanted to bring her daughter to school and stay for a little while." She frowned and shook her head, no doubt thinking about Meg's loss.

"Yes, I heard that Mrs. Stramtussle had died. That must be a terrible shock to the whole town."

"Indeed, it is. But, we're not here to talk about such awful things," the principal said, taking a seat behind her desk and squinting at Allie's paperwork. "It's very nice to meet you, Mrs. Shaw. And hello, Allie. I'm Mrs. Heard, and you're right, you *heard* it here first."

The principal tittered at her own joke as she squinted at us. Allie didn't laugh, but she smiled politely.

"What kinds of things do you like to do?" Mrs. Heard asked Allie, leaning forward to engage with her. Allie shrugged her shoulders.

"She's a little shy," I said.

"No, I'm not," Allie whispered to me. "I just don't want to be here."

"I hope you'll take your time making up your mind about that. Now, we've got you assigned to Ms. Tyler's homeroom. That's your first period. She'll get you set up with a locker and give you the rest of your daily schedule. I think you'll find she's a warm and welcoming person—she's new herself," Mrs. Heard said. Allie nodded, finally making eye contact with the principal. "But, you know, she's going to want you to participate in class, so you better start using that voice of yours."

"Okay," Allie said, trying her best to speak up so that Mrs. Heard could hear her.

"Wonderful. Now, your mom needs to finish some paperwork. Fortunately, we have already received your records from your old school." Allie looked at me, puzzled. Victor and I had dealt with some of the administrative details while Allie and I were in limbo and staying in a motel for a few weeks after we entered witness protection. "If you want, you can go into the yard and meet some of your new classmates. Recess just started for the six, seventh, and eighth graders, so you'll have a little time to get acquainted. We'll see you tomorrow at eight thirty."

Allie did as the principal suggested and went to the playground, though I doubted she'd do much mingling with her new classmates. At least she went out there. It was a start.

I completed and signed the requisite forms with the principal, focusing on making sure I didn't accidentally write our old names. Then I gave her Allie's newly-minted birth certificate, proclaiming her Allison Shaw instead of Alicia Martinez as her original birth certificate had. There was no more Alicia Martinez, just as there was no more Patricia Martinez—that was me, before all of this began—since that horrible night in Las Vegas with Claudia.

She'd always been the wild one, compared to me. She'd left our family at twenty-two, hooking up with a rapper named Caldrón, whose real name was Ricky Sanchez. He met Claudia after she won a backstage pass for one of his concerts from a radio show. That night, she put on her tallest heels, her lowest cut dress, puffed up her hair, and plumped up her lips and went to the stadium where he and his band were performing. Ricky fell for her, and soon Claudia was traveling with him. She stuck with him even as he went through his ups and downs. Had I only understood what had happened to Ricky, I could have done something before our lives were changed forever.

The school bell rang, signaling the end of the break for the middle school kids. I retrieved Allie, who was lurking outside the office door. We headed first to the small market, Al's Food and Booze, which pretty much said it all. According to the little plaque above the door, this had apparently been a grocery store for the last one-hundred-plus years.

I hefted a large bag onto one hip while Allie stuffed a few things into her backpack to carry. As we descended the hill toward our house, I was glad I hadn't purchased more groceries because what we did buy was getting heavier by the minute.

As we came around the curve on the final stretch of our journey, we spotted a sheriff's SUV parked in front of our house. This couldn't be good. As we approached, a cop got out of the car and headed toward us.

"Hello, ma'am. I'm Deputy Sheriff Darla Cotton. Do you have a few minutes to speak with me?" She wore the standard beige uniform shirt with a men's style tie and dark khaki slacks. Her low, tight bun, slender face, and long nose gave her a hawkish look, which I hoped didn't reflect her attitude. If I wasn't mistaken, I'd seen her earlier in the day at the house next door.

"Um, sure, I guess. Come on up." I was trying to be a little more tentative than the usual don't-mess-with-me attitude I'd often had in New York.

"What's your name?" the deputy asked, with a forced-casual demeanor. At nearly six feet tall, she loomed over me, setting me on edge.

"I'm Ruby Shaw, and this is my daughter Allie."

I didn't want to talk with this woman—but it didn't seem like I had much choice. Trying to keep my hands from shaking, I unlocked the front door while juggling a bag of groceries.

"Why don't you come back to the kitchen. I need to put these groceries away," I said. Allie set her backpack down on the kitchen counter and went off to her room, plugging in the headphones for her iPod on the way. "Please make yourself comfortable," I told Deputy Cotton, offering her a chair.

The deputy sat down at the kitchen table while I unpacked the perishables from the grocery bags.

"Looks like you're still getting settled," she said, looking around.

"We just moved in yesterday, so there's still a lot to do. Now, what can I help you with?" I asked as I put a box of half-melted ice cream sandwiches in the freezer.

"As you're likely aware, your neighbor, Mrs. Greta Stramtussle, was found dead in her living room earlier today. I'm checking with the neighbors to see if anyone heard or saw anything unusual."

"Well, it was bizarre. Was there some sort of tour last night? I saw someone with an ax chase a few people out the door of my neighbor's house. The group was initially frightened, but after that, they laughed it off, and the hooded figure went back inside."

"We've got a guy who runs tours. He said there was one last night but didn't mention it had been one of the scarier ones. Derek Stramtussle—"

"I take it he's related to Mrs. Stramtussle? That can't be a common name."

"He's her son. He leads historical tours through town. Paradise used to be a ghost town, you know."

"Yes, I've heard that," I said, trying to be as agreeable as possible.

"Tourists seem to like the spooky tours the best. Derek led the tour last night, but at the time, his mother wasn't there."

"She wasn't hacked to pieces, I hope."

"No, that whole thing with the guy and the ax, that was just Derek's team trying to spice things up to give the tourists a thrill," she let out a little laugh, caught herself, and went back into law enforcement mode.

"Thank goodness," I said, shaking my head. I'd seen too much real violence lately. The image of my brother-in-law, gun in hand, standing over a man lying on the carpet and the ear-splitting sound of the gun firing, shocked me to the core each time I remembered it. I couldn't imagine someone wanting to purposefully scare themselves after the real terror I'd experienced.

"Does this mean you're concerned about the circumstances of Mrs. Stramtussle's death?"

"Until we get word from the medical examiner, we'll assume

she died of natural causes. It's standard operating procedure to ask around, just in case," the deputy said.

"But what's the story with the ax-wielding character?"

"It's an old tale about a man who died when he had his head chopped off in a firewood-cutting accident."

"That seems unlikely," I said, tempering the sarcastic attitude I usually sported as I stuffed a bag of green beans into the refrigerator's crisper.

"Well, yes, it does, but these things happened so long ago, there's no way to know what the facts are. They say a headless ghost haunts this street."

"I don't believe in ghosts, so I guess I don't have much to be worried about."

"The ghost tours have brought in business, though everyone wishes it was more. Well, most people do. Tourists come to town, and they usually stick around and spend some money," the deputy said with a shrug. "This is just a formality, but do you have an alibi for last night?"

"I was here with Allie. She was asleep, so she can't prove I was here."

"Hm. No one else can vouch for you?"

I thought about Victor. He could tell her that he'd dropped me off, but after that, even he couldn't verify what I did after that.

"No, sorry. You'll just have to take my word for it. Now, is there anything else I can do for you, Officer Cotton?" I asked, hoping to hurry the woman out the door.

"That's *Deputy* Cotton."

"Oh, sorry. I wasn't sure how to refer to you." Didn't she have more important things to do than grill me or correct my usage of law enforcement terminology? I certainly did, like putting the rest of the groceries away.

"Thanks for telling me about what you saw last night." Deputy Cotton rose and headed for the front door. I breathed a sigh of relief, knowing my official interrogation was over. "So, you and your daughter just moved in? What do you think of our little town?"

It was too good to be true that the deputy would be done so quickly with her questions.

"We like it so far but haven't had time to see much of anything other than the café, the school, and a quick stroll through downtown." All I hoped now was that the deputy would leave and not start asking questions about where we'd come from.

"It was good to meet you. I'm sorry to have had to intrude on you like this. I will see you around town." It was probably my big-city paranoia talking, but that sounded more like a threat than a promise.

"Yep, maybe so." Did I actually say *maybe so?* I had to remind myself that in this tiny town of five hundred, there was no doubt about it, I'd be running into her much more often than I'd like.

The deputy turned to leave, but paused in the entry.

"So, where are you and your daughter from?" Deputy Cotton asked, her attitude shifting from formal investigation mode to that of a curious neighbor. Of course. Just my luck that I'd have to recite my new background story to a sheriff's deputy who was probably an expert at identifying liars.

"We moved from Colorado." Lie number one. "My daughter was having trouble fitting in there." Lie number two. "I've always loved Arizona, so we decided to try Paradise." Lie number three.

"What kind of work do you do?" Answering this question was going to be more difficult.

"I'm freelance right now—"

"In other words, unemployed," the deputy said. Clearly, she'd heard this before from scoundrels and slackers she'd interviewed.

"I used to work in retail sales, but I'm looking at other opportunities right now." That sounded pretty good. I'd practiced those sentences dozens of times. I hoped she wasn't going to grill me about where we were from in Colorado. I could tell her Winterfield, but more than that, and I was sunk.

"Good luck with that because opportunities here are few and far between. That's how I ended up working for the sheriff's department. There weren't many choices, and I refused to work at the dry cleaners."

Funny, but the dry cleaners seemed like the perfect place to work. Laundry comes in dirty and wrinkled and leaves clean and perfectly folded. The biggest problem was the idea that I'd have to be helpful to dozens of people each day. I didn't always play well with others. That's what I loved about being a studio artist. I could be alone and listen to music and paint with no one to bother me.

"Let me give you some advice. You may hear some buzz around town. It can be gossip central here," the deputy said.

"What do you mean? About me?"

"You arrive, no one knows a thing about you," Darla said with a matter-of-fact shrug. "Not many people are moving here except artists, for the cheap rent and the funky ambiance, and you don't seem to be one of those."

I wished I could tell her the truth. I *was* an artist. But I was an artist in hiding, not able to let my true colors show. A woman was dead, next door to me no less, the same day I moved in. The timing was terrible. I remained hopeful that Mrs. Stramtussle died of a heart attack and nothing more.

"If you think of anything else, give me a call." Deputy Cotton handed me her business card, complete with a fancy crest of the county sheriff's department.

Everything would be better once people got to know me— the new, fictional me. I would have to work on my people skills and my acting skills, or at least my lying skills.

After the deputy left, I went to Allie's room to check on her.

"Why was that cop here?" Allie asked.

"Apparently she's a deputy, not a cop, and she had some questions about what I saw last night and wondered if I'd seen or heard anything."

"What did you see, Mom? You haven't told me anything."

"I just saw something fake—it was like a show, a tour. It wasn't real."

"That cop, she's not going to take us away, is she? Did you break the rules already?" Allie flopped onto the bed, burying her head in a pillow.

"Hey, no, it's not like that. A lady died, and the cops are trying to figure out what happened. It doesn't have anything to do with us." I left out the part where Deputy Cotton mentioned that we might not be welcomed with open arms in Paradise given that we'd arrived unexpectedly, had no particular reason for being here, and our neighbor died the night we moved in. "But hey, just imagine what your room will be like once we fix it up."

"Yeah. It's okay. It'll never be as cool as what I used to have," Allie said, flipping over on her bed to face me and wiping away a tear from the corner of her eye.

"I promise we'll do something to your room to make it much cooler. Maybe we can do some art projects."

"I thought Victor said no art," Allie said as she started to shut down again.

"Maybe Victor doesn't need to know."

FOUR

On Tuesday morning, Allie and I walked to school. She was back to her glum mood, dragging her feet at a snail's pace. There had been only a few glimmers of her old self since we entered the WITSEC program. I dropped her off at the school gates, saying our goodbyes before she trudged off past groups of kids who seemed not to notice her. A pang of guilt hit me hard. I hoped Allie would make a new friend soon. I was sure it would help her feel better about our new normal.

Armed with nothing more than a confident smile, I headed toward the center of town, determined to find a job. Any job.

Up first, the dry cleaners. They had a closed sign on their door, and I guessed there weren't too many people getting their clothes dry cleaned here. Paradise was more of a Laundromat kind of town. While I had initially thought working at the dry cleaners would suit me, now that I could smell the chemicals and burnt starch, I moved past this as an employment option.

This was only the first stop on my mission to find employment. There would be more opportunities, I was certain. I had to keep a positive attitude if Allie and I were going to make it in Paradise.

Business was definitely not booming in town, but the shop owners weren't helping matters. On upper Stewart Street, I passed Jenna's Jewelry and Gems—its window display looked pretty sparse with only a few handmade necklaces and rings. Next was Knitted Treasures—featuring cobwebby balls of yarn and a hand-lettered sign that read, Out to Lunch … For the Rest of the Day. Next on the street was Ceramics and Such—though they had some lovely things in the window, the window itself was grimy, not the most welcoming vibe to get from a shop.

I could do so much to help them if I could only tell them who I really was. I'd had my paintings in several galleries all over the nation. I knew what worked and what didn't when it came to creating a welcoming, customer-oriented gallery where people actually sold things, as opposed to items sitting idly in a window, gathering dust. Unfortunately, I wasn't that person anymore. Who was I to tell any of the shop owners what would or would not work for them? Certainly not me, an unemployed stranger.

Around noon, I stopped at Ferrell's Feed and Tack. It was a long shot but nothing ventured, nothing gained. I talked with a burly man named Sam Ferrell, whose fashion statement was greased-back hair and a dusty gray cowboy hat. He wasn't over-enthusiastic about hiring me, but since he'd had no other candidates, he said he'd give me a chance. I was to be on the job Thursday at nine. That was perfect. I could walk Allie to school, and then follow Copper Canyon Road, which forked off of upper Stewart to Ferrell's Feed.

To celebrate, I stopped by Bette's Place for lunch. Bette, as usual, was keeping her customers happy with efficient and cheerful service.

"Well, well, well, look who the cat dragged in," Bette said.

"I don't look that tired, do I?" I asked Bette with a laugh, as I scoped out my seating options. Not wanting to sit at a table by myself, I took a seat at the counter. Bette sidled up beside me.

"You're becoming a regular, just like everyone else in town. Coffee?"

"Absolutely," I replied.

Bette set up a cup and poured some coffee into it. "What's with the satisfied smile on your face?"

"I found a job," I said, breaking into a grin.

"In this town? Yes, indeed, you are lucky! It seems there aren't too many people looking to hire. There are several shops about to go out of business. They can't hire anyone. Most of them don't have much business sense. Who hired you?"

"I'm starting work at Ferrell's the day after tomorrow."

"Ah, well, I hope that works out for ya, sugar," Bette said, patting my hand.

That didn't sound very encouraging, but perhaps I read her wrong. Bette slid the pitcher of cream and the ceramic dish of sugar packets to me, then rushed off to serve another customer. Without Bette's chatter, I noticed how much quieter it was in the café today than it had been yesterday. Had everyone been talking about me before I'd made my entrance? Or was I imagining things? I pulled over a copy of the local newspaper from the spot at the counter next to me. The paper could at least occupy me until I could finish my coffee and get out of there. My jaw dropped when I saw the headline—"Foul Play Suspected in Local Real Estate Maven Greta Stramtussle's Death."

If the people in the diner weren't talking about me, they most certainly were talking about Mrs. Stramtussle and her tragic end. Fortunately, she and I were only connected by having been next-door neighbors for a few hours. I reassured myself that there was no reason for anyone to assume I had anything to do with her demise.

I choked on my coffee when I got to the line in the article that read, *Mrs. Stramtussle died Sunday night at the age of 71. She was well-known for her Good Samaritan deeds, including breathing new life into this town through a series of real estate deals, and controlling a large feral cat population. Mrs. Stramtussle had recently leased two of her properties located at 33 and 37 Castlerock Road, which had been empty for quite some time. Many of the neighbors were delighted that these two vacant properties were now occupied, even while rumors of their possible demolition remained unconfirmed.*

I was one of the people now living in number thirty-three. If the deputy asked me about my lease, I would have trouble explaining that I didn't have one. I couldn't tell anyone what my rent payment was, or even who I was paying it to, since I was currently not paying anything thanks to the United States government. I would have to be friendly and as unsuspicious as possible until this whole thing blew over. As I drank my coffee, I felt sure that people were stealing glances at me. Talk about a rocky start to living in a new community.

"I see you read about Mrs. S," Bette said, returning to refill my cup. "Looks like it was some sort of home invasion. Poor thing, lost her life and all they took was her diamond wedding ring—and it was a big one ... the diamond, not the ring. Hard to believe, really. I mean, who would want to murder her? Why couldn't they have taken her ring and left her alive? What's the sheriff's department doing about it?"

Bette always had more questions than answers.

As I sat talking with Bette, I watched as the cook took a trash can full of lettuce, carrot tops, and assorted other wilted veggies out the back door and threw the contents in a dumpster. Those scraps were my solution to my crappy soil—I could set up a compost pile. I remember my dad having one on our farm in Clovis. I'd watch him turn it, the steam rising as he did, creating the most fertile soil for our family garden, but never enough for the whole farm.

"Bette? Do you always throw away your vegetable scraps?"

"Sure, no other option around here, I'm afraid."

"Could I take them off your hands?"

"Now, honey, if you and your girl are hungry—"

"No, it's not that. We have plenty of money. I was wondering if I might be able to grow something at my house."

"You mean something more than tumbleweeds? Ha!"

"If I make some compost, I could try to get the soil in good enough shape to be able to start a garden."

"I suppose we could set those scraps aside for you, and you could pick them up."

"If it's more than a grocery sack, I'm not sure how I'd get them down to my house since I don't have a car.

"Maybe Luke, my cook, can bring them down for you—he heads home that way each day."

I peered over Bette's shoulder at Luke. He was six feet tall with wavy ash-blond hair. He sported a few days of stubble on his face, which gave him a rugged look. While he wasn't exactly burly, he seemed solid, firm, and in a word, sexy. As far as I was concerned, he could help me out in many more ways than just bringing me organic matter. But I needed to remember that romance of any kind wasn't in the cards for me, at least not right now. I definitely wouldn't want to keep secrets from someone I was in an intimate relationship with. And—I was getting ahead of myself.

"Sure. That'd be great," I said.

Bette shouted to Luke in the kitchen. "Get over here and meet Ruby!"

Luke smiled and waved. "Sorry, but I'm working on orders for table five," he yelled back, as he flipped an omelet.

"We don't want to interrupt him, then. I'll fill him in, and I'm sure he'll be able to bring you some scraps for your garden real soon."

"Thanks, Bette, I really appreciate it."

"Oh, and if things don't work at Ferrell's Feed and Tack, you could always try my boyfriend's tour business—he runs the Haunted History Tours. Derek might be hiring."

"Derek Stramtussle?"

"You got it. The hottest man in town, and he's all mine."

But Bette had it all wrong. The hottest man in Paradise was working in the kitchen right behind her.

I finished my coffee, paid, and left, all the while thinking about Mrs. Stramtussle. Had everyone in the café started talking about me the moment I'd gone? I wouldn't doubt it. Then again, maybe I was paranoid. But like Jeremy, my ex, used to say, *Just because you're paranoid doesn't mean they're not out to get you.* Then again, I think Jeremy might have smelled a little too much paint thinner in his life to be completely sane. The more I thought about Jeremy, the more relieved I was that he was ancient history for Allie and me.

Excited that I'd found a job, I decided a little retail therapy was in order. There was a shop called the Zen Quilting Company that intrigued me. The building was shaped like a slice of pie, squeezed-in by a sharp hairpin curve that connected the upper section of Stewart to the lower portion of the street in downtown. I stepped inside and discovered that the entire store was full of gorgeous handmade quilts and lightweight batik throw blankets in all the colors of the rainbow. Oh my! To celebrate my new job—granted, I'd not started the job yet—I decided I would splurge on a couple of quilts.

The proprietor, a woman about my age, emerged from the back room. She wore loose-fitting linen pants and a fitted tank top—casual elegance at its finest.

"Hello, welcome. How can I help you today?" The woman's attitude was calm and serene. With the sweet smell of cedar filling the room, I could picture myself staying in this delightful shop all day.

"Hi, wow. I love your shop! Your color choices are amazing."

"Thank you. Is there something I can help you find?"

"I was thinking about getting a couple of quilts. There are so many to choose from, I don't know how I'll select only two."

"We've got a special going right now—buy three, get the

fourth free. You see, we have a lot of inventory right now, so we've been discounting some of our quilts," the woman said as she moved gracefully through the room, showing me some options. "Why don't you have a look around, and call for me when you need my help. I'm finishing up a quilt in the back room. I'm Amber, by the way."

I was like a kid in a candy shop. So many choices! Slowly, I narrowed down my options. I had only planned on getting two quilts—one for each of our beds—but I couldn't pass up picking out two more after Amber mentioned the sale.

I hoped Victor wouldn't be too upset that I spent some of the money he provided on decorative quilts. He'd probably just tease me for spending it on something as silly as beautiful blankets for my new home. To me, they weren't frivolous. If they would help us feel comfortable in our new surroundings, they were worth their cost and then some. The prices on the quilts were actually quite affordable, and even more so with the buy-three discount. If there's one thing a New Yorker loves, it's a bargain. I was a force to be reckoned with at a post-Christmas sale at Bloomingdale's.

I finally settled on two quilts—a turquoise one for Allie's twin bed, and a sage green one for my queen bed, and two throws for the living room in yellows, oranges and golds. The throws I could use on the sofa, or an armchair, if one ever arrived.

I called out to Amber, and she glided over to help me with my purchases.

"Excellent choices," Amber cooed as she gently wrapped each quilt in tissue paper before placing them in a brown paper shopping bag.

The total purchase was surprisingly reasonable. I wasn't sure I could convince Victor of that. Whoever said money couldn't buy happiness didn't know where to shop because at that moment I felt better than I had in weeks. I had a spring in my step as I headed home.

As I entered my house, I was delighted to see an upholstered chair, coffee table, end tables, a TV, and a lamp. The furniture fairies had come through! Everything looked secondhand. As long as we had something better than an empty room, we could be comfortable here.

The chair was a horrible pale brown, my least favorite color —but at least we had another seating option other than the sofa. I'm sure whoever chose it thought beige was a safe choice because it's neutral. I pulled out a colorful throw and flung it over the chair—which immediately improved it. I tossed the coordinating quilt on the sofa. The place was looking better already. What can I say? I hate beige.

I rushed through the house. Allie had a desk and chair in her bedroom. I had a nightstand, but no lamp. I found two boxes of dishes, glasses, pots, and pans in the kitchen.

With some art on the walls, I knew I could turn this house into a home. As Allie had told me on more than one occasion, I could make something out of nothing. She was right; I had those skills. Still, I had to be careful about being too over-the-top with decorating, or else face a scolding from Victor for being too creative. I was already walking a thin line after purchasing my quilts today.

I unstacked two small matching tables that had been made circa 1975 and shoved them into a spot at each end of the couch. I needed a lamp for each end table, but only had one. Rats! I would need a couple more. I'd have to see if I could find some the next time I was in town because you can always use more light in a room.

It was a long way from looking like a home. In fact, it was nothing like my old home—my real home—with its thick Persian carpets in vibrant shades of reds and purples and walls covered with my paintings and those gifted to me by friends.

This place would never be the home I longed for in the city that never sleeps.

The lamp was by far the classiest item supplied by the furniture fairies, an oval bronze base with an etched image of a cat on it and a mica shade. I carried the light to my bedroom and set it on my nightstand, which had been painted white several decades ago. Man oh man, I needed some paint to give that little table a makeover. I ran to the living room and grabbed the shopping bag. I pulled the green quilt out of the sack and tossed it across the bed. It was perfect. I left Allie's still folded in tissue on her bed. I hoped she'd like it, even if it wasn't black.

I called Victor.

"Thanks for the furniture. It looks, um, good." I didn't want to be a snob, but it was basic thrift store quality. I was going to suck it up and be grateful.

"You're welcome. Picked some of it myself. It's been a little difficult sourcing items for your house. Everything else okay?"

"No, actually. How am I supposed to deal with the fact that a murdered woman who lived next door to me owned the home that I now live in? How do I—"

"Whoa, slow down. Let's start with the first part—a murdered woman. Tell me about that," Victor said.

I explained all I could about Mrs. Stramtussle, the house, and the gossip swirling around me, even though I'd only been in this town less than forty-eight hours.

"Do you want me to come and get you two? Move you somewhere else?"

"No. I want to stay. I found a job!"

"Good for you. I knew you could do it."

"I'm not completely helpless, but I could use a little assistance. I've already had to deal with a deputy who came by and asked me a bunch of questions about who we are and why we're here."

"I'm sure you gave her your well-rehearsed answers."

"I did, but now that I live next door to the newly-deceased Mrs. Stramtussle, some of the people in town are suspicious of me. She leased this house and another one on the other side of what is now a crime scene. I show up, and it's a dump—"

"It's *not* a dump—"

"It's not the Ritz-Carlton, that's for sure. Someone murdered this lady. That's the newspaper article's narrative, and I swear, I can feel everyone looking at me like I'm some sort of criminal. Today at the café—"

"I know you're feeling weird. Getting used to having a new identity can be difficult. Give it some time."

"Okay, I will. But please, can you give me some sort of fake lease? Maybe I can use that if that deputy starts asking questions about my living situation."

"I'm sure the deputy knows you're in WITSEC. Our office certainly communicated with the sheriff's department in Wendlewood. Let's see, that guy's name is Ross ... Sheriff Irv Ross. The deputy who's been sniffing around you, I think she's just giving you a hard time."

As I talked with Victor, I wandered out onto the landing outside the back door.

"You know what else? I was thinking about a garden."

"A garden?" I heard amusement in his voice. "You don't seem like the gardening type."

"What's that supposed to mean? I can't do my art anymore, so I have to do something creative. I need a way to occupy my time. I'm serious. I need some potting soil, a shovel, maybe a wheelbarrow."

"Soil? Shovel? Wheelbarrow? These seem like pretty unusual requests for a city girl like yourself."

"Don't ever call me a girl. Seriously. Allie's a girl. I'm a woman."

"It was a figure of speech. Don't get all prickly with me, especially if you want me to fulfill your random requests."

"Got it. I will keep my prickly attitude to myself. Speaking of prickly, though, maybe I could grow cactus! That could be fun. They certainly grow around here." My brain shifted into high gear as it often did when I got excited about a new creative project.

"As long as you don't grow cannabis because that is a big no-no when you're in WITSEC. We don't want you in contact with the wrong kind of people or breaking any laws. Remember, if you commit a crime, you're out of the program. No chance of redeeming yourself."

"Got it. No weed. I wasn't planning on that anyway."

Victor chuckled. "So, you're thinking about cactus?"

"That's right. You know, like succulents. They're so unusual, the shapes and colors and patterns." My creative juices were flowing now.

"Do you know the first thing about growing succulents?"

"No, but I'm a fast learner, and I grew up on a farm!"

"Good luck with your new job, Ruby. Once you show me you can keep it, we'll talk about your gardening supplies," Victor said before saying goodbye.

* * *

I TROTTED down the back steps to look for the jelly jar I'd broken the first night we were here. I was having no luck finding the broken glass, but I ambled through the yard, all the while fantasizing about how I could make this place into a garden oasis. On the next terrace down from where I stood, I saw a glint of glass and made my way down to it.

As I poked at the piece of glass with the toe of my sneaker, I had a horrible realization: This chunk was far too large to be my broken jelly jar.

"Holy crap!" I shouted as I dropped to my knees. Half buried in the rocky soil was a heavy crystal vase, broken into three pieces, and unless I was very much mistaken, a bloody brown smear stained one of the shards. I didn't touch any of it. Instead, I swallowed hard, trying to get a grip. I'd seen such terrible violence only a few short weeks ago, and now there I was, inches from what had to be a murder weapon. It must have been what killed Greta. It was heavy enough to put a good-sized dent in someone's head, and it had what must've been blood on it.

I tried to keep calm. What should I do? I could call Victor back. But then what? He'd tell me this was for the local authorities and scold me for getting into trouble. I hadn't been searching for trouble—I'd been trying to find a broken jelly jar —but trouble seemed to find me at every turn.

I'd promised myself—and Victor—I wouldn't get involved in the death of Mrs. Stramtussle, but living next door to her, and finding what was most likely the murder weapon, made that impossible at this point.

What were my options? I could pretend I hadn't found the vase and leave it here. Law enforcement would eventually start looking for the murder weapon, and they would locate it on their own. After all, it wasn't really hidden, just sitting among a pile of rocks. But pretending I'd not seen the vase could come back to haunt me if I slipped up at some point.

It was also possible that it wasn't the murder weapon. I didn't know how Greta Stramtussle had met her demise. Maybe she had died some other way than being bashed in the head with a crystal vase? The brown streak across one of the pieces of glass did look like blood, so it was very likely that someone hit poor Greta with it.

Truth be told, what I really wanted to do was kick the pieces into the ravine. I doubted anyone would ever find them, and if they did, the three chunks would be in a million pieces. But what was I thinking? I was *not* a lawbreaker. I was an upstanding citizen. Given how I'd ended up in WITSEC, was I truly starting to think like a criminal?

What would make me look the least suspicious? Calling the sheriff's office. I would simply tell Deputy Cotton what I'd found. Easy! I wasn't a suspect, I was an upstanding citizen. I found my phone, sat down on a nearby boulder, and dialed the only deputy assigned to patrol Paradise, Darla Cotton.

"I found something," I told her when she answered, my throat so tight I could barely speak. "I think it might be the murder weapon." I paused and waited with my eyes closed for her response.

"How would you know what the murder weapon is? No one knows that except me, the medical examiner, and the murderer."

"I can assure you I am not a murderer! I found some chunks of a heavy crystal vase in my yard. It's broken, it's got something brown on it ... like blood."

"Hm. I suppose if you were the culprit, you probably wouldn't be calling me," Deputy Cotton said.

"Exactly!"

"But maybe that's what a guilty person would do—call the deputy because that's what they figure an innocent person would do."

"No, seriously, I had nothing to do with this." I glanced at my watch. "I'm sorry, I have to pick up my daughter from school, so I'm going to leave this vase right here for you, okay?"

"I'm off duty today, so I'll make sure someone from Wendlewood comes up to get it. I'm sure they'll want to take a look around. Do you give your permission for some techs to come and collect evidence?"

"Of course I do." They could take as much gravel and rock as they wanted since there wasn't much else. I'd be ever grateful if they found my broken jelly jar.

My hands shook as I hung up the phone. Finding evidence in a murder investigation, when people in town were already suspicious of me, was, in a word, horrible.

Victor wouldn't be happy to hear that I was already entangled in the murder investigation of a neighbor.

Even though I was more apprehensive than ever, I had to hold it together for Allie. Since I didn't want to be late picking her up after her first day at school, I rushed out the door and jogged up the hill.

FIVE

Sweaty and panting, I felt entirely invisible as I waited at the gate after school ended. A few other moms were busy talking or otherwise engaged with their cell phones. But before I started feeling sorry for myself, I realized being invisible was better than sticking out like a sore thumb. I hoped that eventually I'd get to know some of the mothers around town, but right now, I simply wanted to pick up Allie and be on our way.

When Allie came through the gate, I could tell it hadn't been a good day. She shuffled along, head down, separated from the other children.

I pulled her into a big hug as soon as she was close.

"Not here, Mom. Puh-leeze!" she said, pushing past me and charging off in the wrong direction. "Allie! Home is the other direction—downhill, not uphill."

She didn't stop, so I followed. We hadn't explored this part of town yet, so at least it was a new adventure for us. She walked on and on, up and around a switchback onto another steep street. Finally, exhausted, she sat down on a wooden bench in a park on the crest of the hill. I followed her lead.

We sat in silence for a long time and looked out at the valley stretched below us, a mix of red and gray rock and scrubby plants. Finally, Allie spoke.

"They called me Alley Cat," she said, picking at a rock between the treads of her sneakers, not willing to look me in the eye.

"Your name is Allie, so that makes sense. I think it's sort of cute, don't you?"

"No. It's kind of yucky. Like, a couple of hundred alley cats, wild cats, used to live here. That's what some of the kids told me. Until some lady—she has a funny last name, Suntassle or something—killed them all."

"No, honey, I'm sure that's not right. No one would kill cats like that."

I recalled reading in the newspaper how Mrs. Stramtussle had "controlled the town's feral cat problem," but I certainly hadn't thought that meant she'd killed a bunch of cats to do it.

"Besides, it's all so juvenile. I mean, back at home, my friends wouldn't have made up silly names for each other."

"There are worse names than Alley Cat."

"Don't call me that."

"Okay, sweetheart."

As we sat there quietly, we heard a small whimper from the bushes nearby.

"Do you hear that?" I asked Allie. She nodded, jumped up from the bench, and crept toward the bushes.

"Allie! Don't! You don't know what's in there!" But it was too late … she'd crawled into the shrubs on her hands and knees. The whimpering stopped. I dashed to the edge of the plants and crouched down. There was Allie, with a small gray dog in her lap. He happily licked her face, which was likely covered in traces of the turkey sandwich she'd had for lunch. She smiled broadly, her eyes closed, giggling each time the dog licked her. I couldn't remember the last time I'd seen Allie so happy.

"Yuck! No, don't let that dog kiss you—who knows what

kind of germs he has!" Just then, the dog bounded away from Allie. I was crouched down, and as he came toward me, I lost my balance and toppled over. The dog took that opportunity to lick my cheek. "Oh dear. Okay, um. Enough!" I pulled the dog back and noticed that he didn't have a collar. The poor guy must be lost.

"Can we keep him?" Allie asked as she sat down next to the dog, petting him. It was terrific to see happiness, however fleeting, in Allie's eyes.

"I don't know. We're going to have to see if anyone owns him or knows where he came from. So don't get your hopes up. Now, let's get out of here and figure out what to do with this dog."

I took off my jacket, wrapped it around the dog, and picked him up. He weighed about twenty pounds, so he was a bit much to carry. Allie wanted to hold him, but he was a little too wiggly and far too heavy for her. We headed toward downtown. In my earlier explorations, I'd seen a sign for an animal rescue, so we headed down the hill to see if they could help us. Once we'd arrived at lower Stewart Street, I found the building I'd seen earlier.

When I focused on the sign above the animal rescue facility's door, I got a knot in my stomach: *Stramtussle Animal Rescue and Thrift Shop.*

While Mrs. Stramtussle was well known in the community for her work with feral cats, I hadn't realized that extended to creating her own nonprofit animal rescue organization. I couldn't seem to keep away from her. This was what life was like in a small town; I had faint memories of it from childhood. Living in a small town, everyone knows everyone else because there aren't many people to choose from. It was surprising that out of all five hundred people who lived in this tiny town, I kept running into the one person I didn't want to—and she was dead, so it's not like *she* was seeking *me* out. Allie and I stood on the sidewalk, staring in the window. I was contemplating my next move. I didn't want to head inside because that meant one more entanglement with the Stramtussles. But, if we didn't go in, then we'd take this dog home, and Allie would become attached to him. That could be a real problem if he belonged to someone. Just then, a woman inside the shop waved and beckoned us inside. We weren't going to be able to sneak away so easily after all.

Coming through the door, I realized it was Deputy Cotton waving at us. She wasn't in uniform now, so I hadn't recognized her. Out of uniform, with her straight brown hair in a pony tail instead of a tight bun, she looked much more feminine. Her attitude seemed softer as well. Inside the shop, a small kennel area was off to one side, and the rest of the space was chock-full of secondhand furniture and housewares.

"Well hello, you two! Who do you have there?" the deputy asked, pointing to the bundle in my arms. I pulled back the jacket to reveal the small gray dog. "Oh my! Isn't he a cutie!"

"We found him up the hill from the school. Do you know who he might belong to?" I asked.

"If I'm not mistaken, that's Greta's dog. Poor thing—he's so dirty. Let's see if we can get him cleaned up, and I'll be able to tell for sure." She ran some warm water in the sink and soaked some towels in it. Then we each took turns rubbing down the little dog. Once he was clean, we discovered he was, in fact, a white—not gray—dog with a black patch around his right eye. Now that he was clean, he seemed to be feeling better as he wriggled around on the table, enjoying all the attention.

"What do you think? Do you recognize this pup?" I asked.

"Just what I thought. It's Greta's dog. After we found her body, we couldn't locate the dog. We wondered if the culprit had done something with the poor thing. It's great that you found him."

"So, does that mean he needs a home?" I was hopeful that her answer would be yes because I could tell that Allie was as smitten with him as he was with her. Although the fact that, yet again, I'd become entangled with Greta Stramtussle didn't sit well with me. I couldn't see how adopting the dog of a dead woman would land me in hot water, though it seemed these days nearly everything got me in trouble.

"The dog does need a home, and most of us in town have adopted about as many stray pets as we can. So, I'd say he's yours."

Allie filled a bowl with water from the sink and set it down in front of the dog, who happily lapped at it. Allie beamed up at me.

"Does he have a name?" I asked Deputy Cotton.

"I think his name is Ricky."

Ricky wouldn't do. That was Caldrón's name, and I wasn't going to call him that. After all, it was because of Ricky that we'd ended up here.

"Ricky's not our favorite name. We may have to think of something better. What do you think, Allie?"

"His name is Boomer."

"Boomer? Where did you get that name from?" I asked.

"I dunno, it just fits," Allie said with a shrug.

"Okay, then. Boomer it is. What do you say we get him home?"

The deputy loaded a bag with dog food samples for us, along with a secondhand leash, a small foam bed, and some treats. I popped a couple of twenties in the donation box on the front counter, and we turned to go. Sitting next to the front door, I spotted what I was looking for—some terra-cotta pots and hand tools for gardening.

"How much for pots and tools?" I asked. Realizing that between the dog supplies and the gardening materials, it would be challenging to carry everything home. "That rolling tote would come in handy, too."

"Considering you just made a donation and adopted a dog, I'd say you get them all for free," she replied.

"No, I couldn't ... really?"

"They're all yours," Darla replied.

"You don't have any lamps, do you?"

"Sorry, we had a couple, but we sold them."

"Okay, thanks. I have one, but could use a couple more."

"I'll let you know when more come in."

I grabbed the cart and Boomer's bag of essentials, but realized there wasn't room for the gardening supplies. Allie was trying to keep control of Boomer on his leash, and things were getting a little frenetic as I grappled with the rest of the stuff.

"I'd be happy to drop off the tools and planters at your house later if you'd like," Darla said.

"Thanks, that would be terrific. I don't think we can manage it all ourselves." I didn't always welcome help when it was offered. That was part of the New Yorker self-sufficiency I'd cultivated. I needed help now more than ever, and I was thankful for it.

"Plus, I can make sure a crime scene technician from Wendlewood came and picked up that vase from your yard so we can figure out if it's related to the murder of Mrs. Stramtussle."

"Thanks, Deputy Cotton," I said.

"Please, call me Darla."

"Okay, Darla," I said as Allie dashed away with Boomer in the lead. "I'd better get going before I lose those two!"

Darla seemed like a nice person, much more so than the first time we met, and I certainly wanted a friend. But a sheriff's deputy? That seemed a little challenging. Friendship aside, I hoped she might be able to fill me in on her progress with the murder investigation. Ensuring I wasn't a suspect was a top priority of mine. I couldn't help but wonder whether Darla knew the truth about Allie and me. If she didn't know, that uncertainty made the prospect of friendship even more challenging. I knew that the sooner the cloud of suspicion surrounding me was lifted, the better. "So, do you want to stay for dinner when you drop off the pots and tools?" I asked, throwing caution to the wind, hoping I wouldn't regret inviting a deputy into my home.

Darla agreed to dinner, and then we said our goodbyes.

Allie walked ahead of me with Boomer zigzagging in front of her, pulling on his leash. The sadness of her school experience today had faded, and I hoped this little dog would buoy her spirits. I pulled our cartful of dog supplies down the sidewalk, struggling to keep it from running away from me as we made our way home.

SIX

Allie took Boomer to the bedroom while I went to the kitchen to make dinner. I'd decided to make mac and cheese, the ultimate comfort food. I hoped Darla wouldn't be opposed to such a homey choice, but frankly, it was the best I could do on such short notice. I made a salad as well. At least that way we'd have something light and healthy to go along with all those carbs. There were ice cream sandwiches in the freezer for dessert.

While the noodles boiled, I took the opportunity to call Victor and tell him about the suspicious crystal vase I found in the yard. I also had another request for him. These days a computer was essential for day-to-day tasks. I hoped he'd be willing to spring for one, along with a printer. It would be nice to get online and see what was happening in the world on something other than my phone. Victor didn't answer ... typical.

As I started making a salad, the doorbell rang, and I ran to answer, assuming it was Darla. Instead, Victor stood before me.

"What are you doing here? I just called you—you must've already been on your way, right?"

"So many questions." He was right. I sounded like Bette. "Aren't you going to invite me in?"

"Of course. Welcome to my newly furnished home," I said with a dramatic gesture of a maître d'. "Thanks for having more furniture sent over. I really appreciate it."

Victor surveyed the living room. "Not too bad. Livable. Nice blankets," he said nodding at the colorful throws I'd purchased. "I think we did all right."

"I spiced it up with a little color, but not too much, right? I'm going to get some colorful rugs, maybe paint—"

"I understand that you want to express yourself, but let me be clear—you need to be careful about what you do. You're not Painter Patricia anymore."

"I know, I know. I'll shoot for Regular Ruby, how's that? I really am trying. It's tricky though. I have to figure out how to be myself without being my *actual* self."

"You'll figure it out. Most people do," Victor said, settling into one of the armchairs.

"'Most'? What if I'm not one of those people?" I asked.

"You'll be fine. I promise. I can usually tell who will be okay, and I think you and Allie will be fine. You said you called ...?"

"Yes. I did. The first thing, it's not going to make you happy, but it's not my fault." Victor scowled at me but said nothing. I told him about the broken glass vase I'd found in the yard and that I'd called the local deputy who said a crime scene technician from the sheriff's department would come and pick up the evidence.

"Good. Sounds like you did what any upstanding citizen would do," Victor said with a nod. "Let's hope it doesn't get you into hot water."

"I can't imagine it would. I'm an innocent bystander in this whole mess. Another thing is we could really use a computer. Allie's going to need one for school. If not now, then in the next year or so. It would be nice to get online and read some news, watch the occasional cute video. I could check my e-mail."

"E-mail? No one's sending you e-mail. Your old e-mail account is gone."

"Ah. True. I hadn't really thought about that. But still, it would be good to have a computer. I might have someone I could e-mail someday."

"I'll see what I can do."

"I've got a friend coming over. So, you might not want to stick around."

"A friend? You've already got a friend? Who is it?" Victor ignored me and took a seat on the couch.

"Um, her name is Darla." I was unsure if I wanted to tell him I'd befriended a local deputy. But I was a rotten liar, or at least lousy at holding back the truth. "She's works for the sheriff's department."

"A deputy? You really do try to make things difficult for yourself, don't you? She most likely knows your story. The marshals have been in touch with the sheriff in Wendlewood. They know you're here. It's a matter of whether this particular deputy knows what's up with you. I'm sure she'll tell you, and if she doesn't, then she's not in the loop. In that case, she's just like everyone else, stick to your story," Victor said, propping his cowboy-boot-clad feet on the coffee table.

"Don't you dare mess up my new*ish* coffee table." I slapped his feet. "I'm trying to make a friend, you know. Blend in."

"Right, and that deputy is happy to come over and investigate you for the murder of that woman next door."

"I don't think it's like that. You see, we adopted a dog today, and she—"

"A dog?"

"Yes, you know—four paws, barks, etcetera."

"Yes, I know what a dog is. How do you know that your lease allows dogs?"

"I don't. But then again, I've never seen the lease." Victor reached into the interior breast pocket of his jacket and pulled out a couple of pages folded into thirds.

"Your lease, ma'am."

"Thanks. This could be helpful if someone starts asking about my rental of this place. Now, Darla is going to be here any minute, so get going," I said, just as the doorbell rang. Certainly, this time it would be Darla.

"I'd best be on my way," Victor said as I opened the door.

"Hi, Darla. Please come in," I said. She was carrying a crate full of gardening supplies in her arms.

Victor took the crate from Darla and set it on the porch. He nodded a silent greeting at Darla. "Goodbye, Ruby. Catch you later."

Damn him. He was going to leave it to me to explain exactly who he was. I didn't know what to tell Darla. I opted to say he was just a friend.

"Uh-huh. He's quite a nice-looking friend. And tall too," Darla said, giving me a knowing nudge. "He looks familiar. Is he from around here?"

"No, he's not."

"You know, it's awfully slim pickings around here in the potential boyfriend department."

"Is that so? I assure you he is definitely a friend with a lower-case *F*, and definitely not friends with benefits," I said. I'd never considered Victor in that way—he felt more like a big brother to me. But I could see how Darla would find him appealing. He was six foot one and trim, some might even call him skinny, but it suited him. I was terrible at guessing ages, but I'd say he was pushing fifty, though he had the energy of a much younger man. I'd never seen him wear anything other than a plaid dress shirt with the top button undone, a lightweight gray coat, Dockers, and cowboy boots.

His angular facial features gave him an intimidating look,

but when he smiled it was clear he wasn't as serious as he pretended to be. His acerbic sense of humor had taken me a little while to get used to. Ultimately, I knew he cared about all of the witnesses he worked with. Even though he frustrated me more often than not, I had a soft spot in my heart for him.

"If you say so," Darla said with a sly smile. "I brought you the pots and tools, and a housewarming present, one of my favorite plants. It seemed like you needed something to brighten up your new place." She handed me a turquoise-colored pot filled with thick, dark-green pointed leaves.

"Wow, how wonderful! What's it called?"

"It's aloe vera for your kitchen. You can use it to treat burns, plus it's pretty."

"It's lovely, just lovely. Thank you," I said, admiring this fun new addition to my house. I took it to the kitchen and placed it in a sunny spot on the window ledge by the back door.

"You'll have to let me know how to take care of it." Darla was so friendly, but I really had to wonder, was this all part of her plan to determine if I'd murdered Mrs. Stramtussle?

"Sure, you mostly ignore it, water it maybe once a week. You've put it in the perfect location. It should do just fine … Where's Allie?"

"Playing in the bedroom with the dog."

"Is everything going okay?" Darla asked.

"We're still settling in. Boomer is a godsend, actually. He gives Allie something to focus on other than how miserable she is."

"I take it she wasn't too happy moving here."

I didn't want to get into the reason Allie was unhappy about our move, so I took the easy way out.

"You remember what you were like when you were twelve? That's Allie right now. She's so grouchy at times she can't even eat without having a bad attitude."

"I get it. I remember my middle school years. They were the worst, but no worse here than anywhere else, I expect."

"I'm sure everything will be fine. I'm glad we're here," I said, hoping to put the subject to rest.

"We don't get too many people moving here. Of all the places in the world, why did you choose Paradise?"

I decided the best defense was a good offense.

"I could ask you a similar question. Why are you here?"

"My family has lived here since I was a kid."

"No. That's not what I meant. I meant, what are you doing *here*—at my house?" Victor had made me suspicious of Darla. How annoying!

"I see. I came because you invited me. Are you wondering if I'm working on the murder investigation right now?" Darla asked, her face showing no emotion. Was she angry? I couldn't tell. "Well, no. Sheriff's deputies aren't on duty twenty-four seven. Me? I was trying to be friendly. You know, neighborly."

"Neighborly—do you live close by?"

"I've leased number thirty-seven."

This was interesting news. Were suspicions swirling around her in the same way there were around me? Since she was a deputy and a known quantity, having lived in town for most of her life, I doubted it. But still, was she entangled in Mrs. Stramtussle's affairs, and if so, how might that affect her investigation?

If she indeed was the one who killed Mrs. S, might she try and frame me, so no one suspected her? Since she was a deputy, it would undoubtedly be easy for her to do. I'd heard of dirty cops in New York, but I was surprised that it could happen in small-town America. And there she was in my house. My paranoia was escalating.

"So, how is the murder investigation going?"

"I'm going to be completely honest—you're a person of interest in this investigation. Derek Stramtussle said he saw someone lurking around the night his mother was murdered while he was leading the tour. No one else was down here other than you."

"But other people were here the night Mrs. Stramtussle died —her son Derek and all the people on the tour—"

"Right, but they all have alibis."

"The guy with the ax—he was alone. I saw him."

"I'm in touch with Derek Stramtussle regarding who was working for him that night. At one time or another, many of us in the community have worked on his tours—it's really a blast, actually," Darla said, then shifted gears. "You've got no alibi and we found the murder weapon on your property."

"Correction. *I* found the murder weapon and called you. I think I get some credit for that."

"I came here to have dinner with you. I'm not investigating anyone right now. I'm giving you the heads up that you shouldn't plan on going anywhere, and you should keep being the upstanding citizen you claim to be."

"I hear you loud and clear. Does the fact that I'm a suspect have anything to do with people not being super warm and friendly? Last time I was at Bette's Place, everyone stopped talking as soon as I walked in the door."

"You just need to be around a while, and once this murder case is put to rest, people will know you're innocent—you *are* innocent, right?" I thought I saw a glimmer of a smile on her face.

I nodded. "Yes, I am."

"Then, everyone will come around. But it also means I've got to find the killer—that would help all of us."

We would all feel a lot safer if we knew that we didn't have a murderer running loose in our town. But had I to wonder if she meant more than bringing a killer to justice. She certainly had to know that suspicion fell on her because of her real estate dealings with Mrs. Stramtussle. Clearing her name would certainly help her in the same way it would help me. And it might help Darla's career if she solved the case—since it didn't seem like she had much tenure with the sheriff's department.

"Maybe I can help? The faster I'm declared innocent, the easier time I'll have fitting in, right? We'll all be relieved that the murderer has been apprehended."

"We'll see, okay?"

Darla pulled a wine bottle out of the tote bag slung across her shoulder. "I also brought this."

"Oh! You didn't need to do that! But I'm glad you did," I said, taking the wine bottle from her.

"It's local—we've got some good vineyards around here, believe it or not. This is one of my favorites."

I took a look at the label, which had the image of a wild boar on it.

"Sangiovese, one of my favorites. But what's a javelina?" I asked, looking at the label decorated with a hairy pig.

"Javelina, it's one of our best wineries around here. It's a wild pig, actually a peccary. You've never heard of one before?"

"Nope. Can't say that I have."

"Really? Because I thought they had javelinas in Colorado. Isn't that where you said you were from?"

"I am. We lived in Denver—not too many wild animals in the streets unless you count the frat boys who come into the city from Boulder." Whew! That sounded pretty good. I had intended to tell everyone we were from a small town. I racked my brain to recall if I'd told anyone that I was from Winterfield, population ten thousand. I didn't think I had, fortunately, so I didn't need to worry about keeping my story straight yet. The biggest problem now was the likelihood that someone had lived in Denver; there was a much higher chance of that than someone being familiar with Winterfield.

I searched through the drawers, looking for a wine bottle opener before realizing the wine had a twist-off cap. That was a relief because I had no idea if I even had a corkscrew. I located two globe-shaped wine glasses in the box of dishes on the counter, another gift from Victor's team. After washing the glasses, I poured the wine.

"Cheers," I said, holding up my glass and clinking it against Darla's. We smiled at each other, but mine felt forced. I still wasn't used to interacting with others in my new persona. I hoped this constant anxiousness would eventually subside.

"Cheers," she replied. "Did you get rid of a lot of stuff before you moved here?" she asked.

"I did some major purging. I didn't really want to bring a lot with us. Are you going through that right now as you get ready to move?"

"Not really. I don't have much to begin with. I've been living in a cottage below my parents' house. There wasn't much space to accumulate housewares, plus when I have extra things, I tend to take them to the thrift shop."

A timer buzzed in the kitchen.

"Oh! I nearly forgot my mac and cheese!" I ran to the oven and pulled it out. It was perfect—the ideal combination of browned and gooey. I tossed the salad with some oil and vinegar while the pasta rested for a few minutes on the stove. While Darla set the table, I went to fetch Allie. Tapping lightly on the door, I called her name.

"Allie? Are you ready for dinner?" I asked.

"Yeah," Allie said, dropping a rope toy and getting up from the floor where she'd been playing tug-of-war with Boomer.

"Maybe we should leave the door open so the dog can come out and visit." Allie and I went to the kitchen, and Boomer followed us.

As he snuffled around on the floor it was clear he hoped to take care of anything that happened to fall off the table.

"I hope everything's going well with your new dog," Darla said.

"Yeah, he really likes to play—oh, and to chew on things. I had to rescue my iPod before he left teeth marks on it," Allie said, a note of shock in her voice.

"You're going to need to get more chew toys. And you'll need a vet at some point. We've got exactly one in town. Dr. Dan Sweet. He's on lower Stewart, just past the thrift shop," Darla told me.

"Thanks. I'll have to check in and see if Boomer is up to date on his shots. I hope I won't ever need to take him in for surgery to remove an iPod from his belly," I said with a laugh, though I was truly worried about the possibility of huge vet bills if Boomer kept chewing on all the wrong things.

After our main course, I passed around ice cream sandwiches, and Allie told us a little more about school. She really opened up, but when she got to the part about how the kids called her Alley Cat, she looked down at her empty plate and stopped talking. Her new nickname still bothered her.

"Oh—the nicknames! Everyone ends up with one around here. It's actually a good sign your classmates gave you one so soon," Darla said.

"Really?" I said, baffled these silly names were normal here. We didn't do nicknames where I came from unless you were in a gang and had a name like Big Eddie, or in the case of Ricky, you had a stage name like Caldrón.

"When I was in school, I was Darla the Marlin—it made no sense to me then, and still doesn't."

"A marlin? I don't get it," Allie said with a confused smile, looking at each of us in turn.

"You know, a big fish with a pointy nose," I said. Allie stifled a laugh. She couldn't help herself. While Darla didn't look very fishy, she was quite tall and did have an impressively pointy nose. I couldn't help myself and laughed out loud.

"You'll eventually learn everyone's nicknames. I'm not

worried one bit about you," Darla said, making her final judgment as she rose from the table and cleared our plates.

After dinner, Darla asked me if she could go down to the yard to take a look around. I didn't like this shift from a visiting friend to a law enforcement professional, but there wasn't anything I could do about it.

"I heard from the team down in Wendlewood. They came and collected the pieces of the vase you found," she said as we descended the wooden stairs to the yard. We looked out at the desolate landscape beyond the small porch where we stood. "So, where'd you find the vase?"

"Over there," I said, pointing to a rocky spot between the two houses. "I figure whoever chucked the vase over here was hoping the house was vacant and that it wouldn't be found for quite some time."

"Or had hoped to come back for it later to get rid of it," Darla said. "Or maybe they hoped it had rolled all the way down into the gulch and would never be seen again."

I swallowed hard, recalling that I had considered doing that very thing but had opted instead to be an upstanding citizen and called Darla. I wondered, even now, if I should have done that. Kicking the vase down the hill might have made my life much simpler.

SEVEN

Thursday was a big day for both of us. I was starting my first day at Ferrell's Feed and Tack and Allie had a placement test to confirm she was in the right grade. She'd always done well in school, but still, she was nervous. I was confident she'd do fine on the test since she'd been at such a terrific school in New York. We bustled around getting ready for the day and then headed out the door, each of us with bagged lunches. She wasn't the only one who was feeling nervous this morning.

I attempted to give Allie a hug at the school gate, but she stepped back and went reluctantly inside before I could. After dropping Allie off, I headed up the hill to Ferrell's.

Sam Ferrell was a big man with a bigger laugh. He seemed amused by me and puzzled I'd be willing to work at his farm supply store. How challenging could it be? I'd ring up purchases for customers and send them to the warehouse to pick up their items. I'd worked at a hardware store; it couldn't be much different than that. Besides, this would be a great way to meet a few more people and perhaps do a little investigating because the sooner the murderer was found, the sooner Allie and I could settle into town. I could stop worrying that Victor was going to pull us out of Paradise and move us somewhere new.

As I clocked in for the day, I realized I had no idea what time my shift ended. I would have to leave at three to get Allie from school, so I hoped that wouldn't be a problem. I definitely needed to find a babysitter who could take care of Allie after school. Though she might be old enough to be at home without me, I wasn't quite ready for that, and I wondered how Allie would feel.

I hadn't been aware that in addition to ringing up purchases, I'd also need to load some of the supplies for customers if other employees were working in the warehouse or on break. I kicked off my first day on the job with a struggle when I tried to load two thirty-pound bags of manure in the back of a man's truck. He looked familiar, and finally, I placed him.

"Hi, I met you—sort of—at Bette's Place. You're the cook, right?"

"Yes, ma'am. I'm Luke." He held his hand out, and I took it in mine. Oh, it was a large, strong hand, unlike the men I'd dated in the past. They'd either been manicured single dads from Allie's school or artist types with too much paint under their fingernails.

"And I'm Ruby. Nice to meet you. This is my first day on the job."

"Seems an unusual job for a woman."

"What do you mean by that?"

"It's a lot of hard work."

"What makes you think I'm not up to the task?" I asked as I struggled to pull the heavy bags off the top of the pile just out of reach.

"Here, ma'am, let me get those for you."

"I. Can. Do. It," I said, valiantly pulling down a bag and plopping it at my feet. Or more precisely, letting gravity do its thing. "And don't call me ma'am."

Luke grabbed the bag from the ground, effortlessly heaved it into his truck, then grabbed another bag and did the same. Impressive.

"And one of those pitchforks," Luke said, showing me his receipt with the purchase details on it. Fortunately, I knew where the tools were stored, and I was back in a minute with his item. "Here you go. Just curious, but do you have a farm? I'm interested in seeing what people grow around here. I've been thinking about planting a garden, but I'm not sure what to start with." I might as well chat up a handsome dude. It was a perk of the job—perhaps the only one.

"Yeah, I've got a couple of acres down past Castlerock Road, on Grimly Flats, just outside of town. Do you know where that is?"

"Sure. I actually live on Castlerock."

"You're in one of Greta Stramtussle's houses?"

"That's us. My daughter and me."

"I hope that doesn't cause you too much trouble. I don't go in for gossip. I try to mind my own business and cook, but I hear things."

"What kind of things?"

"That you rented that place sight unseen and weren't happy with it once you moved in."

"Who told you that? That's simply untrue. Now granted, it needs some upgrades, but we're going to make it work. Besides, even if the house was a disappointment, I *really doubt* I'd kill her because of it," I said, laughing at my own sarcastic joke.

"You *doubt it?*" he asked, clearly confused. He didn't get my humor.

"No, I was just joking. I definitely wouldn't kill her. I didn't even know her."

Luke laughed softly.

"It's all good. I've got to get back to the café. We had a little lull in business—that's been happening a lot lately—but Bette's probably having a fit by now. Nice to meet you." Luke tipped his baseball hat.

"Hey, if you hear anything about me, will you let me know?"

"I doubt it."

"Huh?"

"I was just joking. Of course. Here's a little warning. Folks around here have a lot of history with each other—good and bad. You'd best be careful."

I waved as Luke drove off. His advice—'you'd best be careful'—sounded nearly like a threat. I had to wonder what he knew that might get Deputy Cotton pointed in the right direction and away from me.

Next, I unloaded a container of chicks that a local rancher dropped off to sell. A peek in the flat rectangular box revealed dozens of adorable yellow baby birds, all squeezed together. Sam told me to put them into an empty metal trough already equipped with heat lamps. I had trouble getting all those little buggers into their new home and spent several minutes gathering up a few of the chirping fluff balls that tried to hide under a nearby pallet. They were all so cute, it made me want to bring a dozen home. But since I didn't know the first thing about raising chickens, I put that idea on the back burner for now.

Although those were difficult tasks, I did my best to do them with a smile on my face. Then came Sally Graber, who needed three bales of hay for her alpacas. She was standoffish with me when we'd first met in her shop, and today her attitude hadn't improved.

"Hi. Nice to see you again," I said, trying my best to be friendly. "My daughter loves the shirt we bought at your boutique. How's everything going with your new online shop?"

"As well as can be expected," she said. The sour expression on her face told me things were either not going as well as she was willing to admit or that she didn't like me one bit.

"You know, it seems we have gotten off on the wrong foot." I decided I'd try a bold and direct approach. "Is there some way that I've upset you?"

"Me? Upset? No. I'm wondering why you're here."

"I came here ..." This answer was always the most difficult. I'd come up with a good story about *who* we were, *where* we used to live, but I was still working on the answer to the question of *why* we were here. "We needed a new start. This seemed like a nice place." It was the truth. We did need a new start.

"It seems pretty risky to come here without a job. You were looking for employment at my shop just the other day."

"As you can see, I'm now employed." I held my arms out and looked around as if I'd just realized I was in a fantastic new workplace.

She wasn't amused. "Greta was my best friend. She never told me who she rented to. Never even told me why she decided to rent those houses. And so, she rented to you, an unemployed, single mother." She raised a judgmental eyebrow.

"I didn't know her." I couldn't explain how I'd ended up in that house, that it had been the one offered to me. "A friend of mine helped me with the lease."

"It wasn't listed for rent. So somehow, you were connected to her."

So much for my how-could-I-be-involved-in-Mrs.-Stramtussle's-murder-if-I'd-just-moved-in-and-never-met-her explanation.

Sally huffed a little and ended our conversation when Sam arrived to do the heavy lifting. I appreciated his help with the bales of hay since there was no way I could have lifted them myself.

I hadn't made a new friend in Sally, but she certainly did confirm that she—and likely others in the community— believed me to have some past association to Mrs. Stramtussle. I had no idea how I could prove a lack of connection. That was going to be tough.

A few minutes before three, I went to the break room to retrieve my purse, having stored it under the counter by the sink. I'd already told Sam I was leaving early since I hadn't set up after-school care for Allie. I stooped down to pull out my handbag, and when I stood up and turned around, there was Sam—a little too close for comfort.

"I'm sorry I have to leave early today. I'll make it up to you," I said, stepping around Sam and heading for the door. He stepped into my path.

"Now, I've got your promise on that? I can think of at least ten ways you could make it up to me." A grin broke across his face, more lecherous than happy.

"I beg your pardon?" I said, standing up to my full height and looking him straight in the eye. I'd learned a long time ago that the best way to deal with someone like this was with fierceness, not finesse. Sam reached his arm around me and touched the small of my back, trying to pull me toward him.

I grabbed his hand and tried to push it away. It was firmly planted.

"You'd better take your hand off of me this instant or you will regret it," I said, pointing my index finger at his nose and raising my voice several decibels. All the other employees were out in the warehouse, so it was unlikely someone would be coming to my rescue.

"Ah, I didn't mean nothing by it." And he used double negatives. It was getting worse by the minute. Sam stuck out his lower lip in a bit of a pout. "Come on now, you couldn't have thought I'd hire you because of all you knew about the feed and tack business—"

That's when I kneed him in the balls.

He curled up like a jumbo shrimp, releasing me and staggering back to lean against the break room counter, all the while gasping out every cuss word he could think of.

"Don't bother comin' back tomorrow," Sam spat as I hurried out the door with my head held high and my purse slung across my shoulder.

EIGHT

Outside the store, I leaned against the fence and caught my breath. I hadn't administered that kind of damage to a man since my first landlord offered me a rent reduction in return for a few sexual favors, a transaction I had declined. I made sure I paid him on time each month for fear of a redux of that lousy interaction.

What was I going to do now? How could I tell Victor? And what could I tell Allie? I'd told her to be friendly and try to fit in. But I hadn't taken my own advice. This wasn't an auspicious start to my career as a non-artist. One day on the job and I was fired—one single day. To make matters worse, I'd have to restart my job search.

I gritted my teeth as I hustled to school. Sam Ferrell wasn't going ruin things for us. Allie was sitting on the steps outside her classroom, her forehead pressed against her knees. This wasn't a good sign.

"Hi, sweetheart. I'm sorry I'm late. I had a little problem at work."

Without a word, Allie handed me a slip of paper. It was a note from Allie's teacher with a recommendation. Based on

Allie's poor test results, she would be moved from seventh grade down to sixth.

"Allie, what's this all about?" The day suddenly had gone from bad to worse.

"I dunno, Mom. I ... I—"

"I'll be right back." I opened the classroom door and marched inside. I was already frazzled from what had happened at the feed store only minutes ago, so I was about to explode as it was.

"Excuse me," I said, making a beeline for Ms. Tyler, who was erasing the whiteboard at the front of the room. "Can we talk about Allie's test scores?"

"Yes, Mrs. Shaw, I hated for you to find out this way, but Allie assured me that sending a note home with her would be the best way for you to find out since you were working and might not be able to talk with me right after school."

"Here I am." I paused, hands on my hips, and waited for her to explain what happened.

The teacher smiled blandly and put her eraser down. With no explanation forthcoming, I carried on.

"I don't understand. How could Allie have done so poorly on her placement test that you would recommend she be moved back a year?"

"Sometimes, that happens when a child moves to a new school. At times, the curriculum at the previous institution is subpar, and we have to make adjustments."

Subpar. Subpar! I could barely control myself. I kept those words in my head, not spouting out of my mouth, at least not yet.

"I can assure you, Ms. Tyler, that there was nothing subpar about Allie's last school. She was enrolled at—" And then I stopped in my tracks. I couldn't say it. I couldn't say that she had been enrolled in one of the country's best private elementary schools. I swallowed hard, keeping my indignation locked inside. "Uh, yes, I could see how that could happen. Thank you for your time." I turned to go, seething, but unable to express it.

I left the classroom feeling torn apart. For the first time in a very long while, I wished I had a partner, someone who could help me through this challenging parenting stuff and maybe punch a sexual harasser in the face for me.

"Come on, sweetheart, let's go home," I said, holding out my hand to her. Allie grabbed it and pulled herself up, but dropped it as soon as she was standing. "Actually, I think the first stop should be Bette's Place. I don't know about you, but I could really use an ice cream sundae."

Bette was at the café, as usual, pouring coffee and peppering everyone with questions.

"Hello, you two! How was work? How was school? And what can I get ya?"

"We'd like two hot fudge sundaes, please, with rainbow sprinkles." I looked at Allie, "Does that sound all right?" Allie nodded. I knew it would ruin both of our appetites for dinner, but I didn't really care right now. I was glad we only had to answer the last of Bette's questions because the answers to the first two were more troubling.

While we waited, I asked Allie about the placement exam.

"What happened? Did you have trouble with the test?"

"I don't want to talk about it," she grumbled, dropping her head as if she'd found something fascinating in her lap.

"Come on, you know we need to be a team on this. How about I tell you about my terrible day, and you can tell me about yours?"

She nodded and at that moment, Luke arrived with two hot fudge sundaes festooned with rainbow sprinkles.

"Here you go. Bette asked me to drop these off before I head out. I brought you a few extra sprinkles on the side in case it was an extra sprinkles kind of day." Luke gave us each a small nod and a smile before heading for the door.

"I don't know about you, but I could definitely use some extra sprinkles," I said, picking up the little metal sauce cup beside my sundae and tossing some sprinkles on my dessert. "And how about you? Could you use some?"

Allie nodded, finally looking up to admire her sundae. I reached across the table and sprinkled a few rainbow-colored candies on her head, like fairy dust.

"Mommmm," Allie sighed. "That's not what I meant." As she shook her head, the sprinkles cascaded from her light-brown hair and tumbled to the floor. Allie took her tiny metal cup of rainbow bits and dumped the whole thing on the top of her ice cream.

"That bad of a day?"

"Yeah, but I guess part of it's my fault."

"What do you mean?" I asked.

"I, uh, kind of didn't do my best on the test." She pushed the ice cream around in its bowl with her spoon, not making eye contact with me.

"Why, sweetie? Was there something wrong? What's going on?"

"I was kind of, I don't know, insulted. How come I even needed to take this test? I mean, can't they just trust that I'm supposed to be in the seventh grade?"

"Some schools are better than others, so they need to check it out when a new student arrives. It's no big deal. Maybe that fancy school wasn't as wonderful as we thought."

"My old school was great. I miss it, and I miss my friends too. I … I kind of think that test was dumb." Allie took a big bite of ice cream.

"Are you telling me you *tried* to do poorly on the test? Allie Elizabeth Shaw, you better come clean or, or—I don't know what. But I can say this will be the last ice cream sundae you'll see for a while."

Allie took a few more fortifying bites of ice cream and promptly changed the subject.

"So, Mom, how was your first day at work?"

I wanted to tell her how rotten it had been, but she wasn't getting off the hook so easily.

"I'll tell you after you tell me why you purposefully failed that test."

"I thought maybe they'd realize this wasn't a good school for me, and I'd get to go back to the Hawthorne Academy."

I tipped my head back, closed my eyes, and took a deep breath to gather my thoughts. When I opened my eyes and brought her back into focus, I realized where this was coming from. She wanted to go back to how it had been. I reached across the table with both hands and grasped hers.

"Sweetheart, I'm sorry. I've tried to give you everything you need, tried to make a good life for you. I'm sorry we're here. But we're here to stay, for as long as we need to be."

"I'm sorry, Mom. I just was desperate, you know?"

"I know, kiddo, I know." I released her hands. "I also know that if we don't finish this ice cream soon, we're going to have to drink it with a straw."

We both dug into our sundaes. And as we did, couldn't let go of the idea that Allie should be able to retake the test, now that she had admitted she'd failed on purpose.

"You know, there's no time like the present to put something to rest. I'm going back to school. Maybe it's not too late to see the principal about your test," I said as I slurped down the last bit of melted ice cream from the bottom of the bowl.

"No, please, don't. I don't want my mom to have to do everything for me."

"Sorry, I need to do this. You don't have to come. Why don't you stay here and do your homework? I'll be back in no time."

Bette came and cleared the dishes, and I checked with her to make sure it was okay to leave Allie at the table while I went back to the school.

"It's no trouble at all as long as she doesn't plan on sleeping here tonight," Bette said with a cackle as she wiped down the table.

"Stay put, and I'll be back soon." Allie reluctantly pulled a notebook from her backpack.

I race-walked to the school, barely even panting by the time I arrived at the principal's office. I stormed by an open-mouthed Meg at the reception desk—no one was going to stop me now—then barged into the principal's cramped office. Mrs. Heard looked up from her work, startled to see me standing in her doorway.

"So, how can I help you?" The principal's surprised expression shifted to a calm demeanor, which I'm sure she used in most confrontational situations with parents.

"I would like to discuss Allie's placement test."

"Ah, yes. I heard from Ms. Tyler that Allie's scores were considerably lower than expected for her assigned grade."

"Yes, I know that. Allie confessed to purposely doing poorly."

"Why in heaven's name would she want to do that?" Mrs. Heard asked.

"It's a long story," I said, hoping against hope that she'd let it go at that.

"I've got time," Mrs. Heard said, folding her arms, leaning back slightly in her chair, and looking at me over the top of her silver glasses.

I took a seat across from her and explained that Allie was missing her old school and had hoped that by doing poor work this school wouldn't want her and that perhaps she'd be able to return to her old school.

"Hm, that seems irrational," she said, uncrossing her arms and pulling what must've been Allie's test from a folder.

"You work with middle school kids every day, you know

they're not the most rational people," I said, leaning forward, my palms on the desk, hoping to get a glimpse of the test.

"That's true, but we do have guidelines for these tests. Each child is tested once per year, and your child has had hers. We'll be moving her to sixth grade on Monday," Mrs. Heard said, placing Allie's test scores back into the folder with finality.

"This is unfair! Absolutely outrageous! I can't believe you, you—" I shouted, leaping up from my chair.

"Now it seems that it's not just the middle schoolers who are being irrational. I'm sorry, Mrs. Shaw—"

"It's *Ms.* Shaw," I said, ready to snap. "There is no Mr. Shaw!"

"Noted. Unfortunately, I cannot help you with this. If you'd like to take it up with the school board, they may be able to accommodate your request in some way. You'll need to get on the agenda. Talk with the school board president, Sam Ferrell. He can help you out. He owns the feed and tack on Copper Canyon Road. Do you know him?"

My heart sank. I most certainly knew him, but I wasn't going to tell her, nor would I mention that I'd recently injured more than his pride. Speaking of which, it occurred to me that everyone in town was going to know by nightfall what I'd done to him if they didn't know already.

"Fine! That's just fine," I said, punctuating the second *fine* with the slam of a door as I left.

That couldn't have gone any worse. I strode past Meg more slowly than I had minutes before. She raised her hand in a half-hearted wave, and I kept on moving.

NINE

"Well?" Allie finally asked as we headed home.

"I'm going to see what I can do to get you retested, but it's not looking likely." I didn't want to explain that the man who could decide which grade she was in was also the man who I'd injured today when he tried to grope me. "Honey, it might be that you need to do some really good classwork to prove to your teacher you should be in seventh grade, but in the meantime, you're going to have to make the best of this bad situation. I'm going to try and fix it, but it might not happen. I'm sorry."

As we opened the front door, Boomer leaped out at us. He was the happiest dog in the universe, dancing around our feet as if we'd been gone a week instead of a day.

"He probably needs a walk so he can do his business," I said, grabbing his leash, clipping it onto him, and heading for the door. "You coming?"

"No, that's okay. I'm going to finish my homework." I looked at my daughter with my hands on my hips giving her the side-eye. "And I'll make sure I do a perfect job."

"That's my girl!"

Boomer was happy, trotting obediently down the street with

me. Kudos to Mrs. Stramtussle for having trained him well. Living in an apartment meant we'd never had a dog. While I'd had dogs growing up, I'd never trained one. I was relieved that Boomer had already gone through all of that.

I headed downhill and stood in front of the house next door where Mrs. Stramtussle had been killed. Its front door was sealed with crime scene tape.

As I stood there, staring up at the house, I was startled by a voice behind me.

"Returning to the scene of the crime?"

I turned to see a man getting out of an older black station wagon. His face was pallid with a dark, skinny mustache running along his top lip. He looked a little too much like Gomez from *The Addams Family* to make me feel comfortable.

"I beg your pardon?"

"You're Ruby Shaw, aren't you?"

"I am. And you are …?"

"Henry Villanueva."

"And how do you know me?"

"Because in a town our size, it's big news when someone new moves in. I own the Hilltop Hotel. It's up there at the top of the hill, as you might imagine." He laughed a little at his joke as he pointed to the towering hill that loomed above us.

"Nice to meet you. We haven't made it to the top of the hill yet." I looked in the direction he was pointing, but couldn't really see much more than a brushy hillside.

"It's haunted, you know. It's quite popular with the tourists," Henry said. He was completely serious.

"Ah. I've heard there are hauntings." I decided to stay neutral on the subject. I didn't want to offend someone who could be a future employer. "I'm looking for a job. Any chance you have an opening?" I asked.

I liked the idea of working at a hotel, even a haunted one, though I couldn't believe that was really true. There would be interesting travelers coming in from all over the world. I could help customers discover the unique sights in the area. It sounded exciting, more so than many of the other employment options in this town.

"I'm afraid not. I've got a couple of part-time employees, and we're able to cover all the shifts. If something comes up, you'll be the first to know."

"Thanks. I appreciate that."

"I hope you're able to get settled and enjoy our little town. I know I speak for the rest of the community when I say we're glad these properties aren't sitting empty anymore."

"Empty? Didn't Greta Stramtussle live in one of them?"

"She used to live in this middle one, but for the last few years she's been in a little cottage behind the animal shelter on lower Stewart."

"But why didn't she want to live in this perfectly good house?"

"She wanted to be downtown, close to the animals she was working with. Plus, the walk into town can be a bit of a challenge."

"I agree with that. I'm going to be in the best shape of my life after trudging up and down this hill each day."

"Perhaps you should drive."

"No car. Besides, I don't know how I'd manage driving through those switchbacks. I'd probably go so slow it would be faster for me to walk." Granted, being a New Yorker, I didn't drive much—cabs and the subway were my preferred modes of transportation. Of course, I'd not find either of those in Paradise.

"It's not too scary. Those big tour buses can't make it up these narrow switchbacks, but regular cars can handle it, if the driver takes their time." He gestured toward the zigzagging road. "There are a lot of people in town who think knocking down these houses to make room for a new tour bus depot would be a good idea. The idea that floated around town was that buses would park down here and then small vans would shuttle tourists into town. Now the house is a crime scene, who knows when that mess will be cleared up? And we've got you living in one, and Darla is moving into another."

"Wow, I guess I messed up your plans for a parking lot."
There I went, shooting off my mouth again!

"Oh, I'm not one of the people who wants to see these gems torn down."

"I'm sorry, I didn't mean to sound so rude. My daughter and I have had a bit of a rough time so far getting settled in."

"You just need to meet a few more people. Maybe you can see your way clear to meeting some of the folks at the Haunted Hayride. It's something new Derek Stramtussle is developing— an event that might draw tourists to our little hamlet. Several of us have volunteered to make our own scary vignettes that everyone will see during the hayride."

"That sounds like fun. Not too scary for my daughter, I hope?"

"It's basically an outdoor haunted house. I expect your daughter will be fine. It's tomorrow evening at seven. Just go to the bottom of the road here, and turn right on Grimly Flats."

Henry slid into the driver's seat, put his car in gear, and cruised off, a little faster than I thought was safe, up the hill toward his hotel.

Ideas swirled through my head—someone, I wasn't sure who —wanted to rip out these three houses and put in tourist bus parking. I'm sure Greta Stramtussle made it a much more diffi-cult prospect by leasing the properties out. She was the owner, so she had every right to do with them as she pleased. But who would want to raze these houses and turn them into a parking lot? Who would be angry enough with her to kill her over her decision?

I also wondered who Mrs. Stramtussle was meeting at her

house the night she was killed. That person certainly seemed like they would be suspect number one. I wasn't sure how I was going to figure that out. By process of elimination, who *wasn't* meeting Mrs. Stramtussle that night? And while I didn't think I'd be able to eliminate all 497 residents of Paradise—I knew it wasn't Allie or me and Greta hadn't killed herself. I hoped I might at least be able to give Darla a list of suspects to consider. Of course, if Darla were trying to frame me for murder, there wasn't much I could do to stop her from doing just that, other than finding the real killer and getting them to confess.

I walked to number thirty-seven, the house Darla was moving into and stood in front of it for a long while. It looked exactly like mine, a little shabby around the edges.

Then I kept going. Another hundred yards past Darla's rental, Grimly Flats Road forked off to the right and on the road's far side, a farm. That must be the farm where Luke lived and worked when he wasn't cooking at Bette's Place. I turned and headed for home, encouraging Boomer to take every opportunity to do what he needed to do along the way.

As I came up the street, a black sedan that I'd recognize anywhere was parked beyond our house. Victor was back. He was probably checking on me again. As I approached the passenger side door, Victor rolled down the window. I peered inside, my breath catching in my throat.

Staring back at me was Claudia, though she looked a little different than the last time I'd seen her. She was gaunt as if the stress of all that had happened in the previous few weeks had eaten away at her. Her hair had been cut short and was darker than it had once been, and I wondered if that was because she needed to change her appearance to be in the WITSEC program, as I had done.

"Claudia! What are you doing here?" I asked, reaching in the window and grasping her in a hug.

"I wanted to see you before I got assigned my new location.

I'm never going to see you again, and I wanted to say ... to say ..." Claudia choked up, got out of the car, and hugged me tightly. "I'm so very sorry for everything. I mean *everything.*"

"Shhhh. It's okay. Allie and I will be fine. Things are going to work out for us. But what about you? Where have you been?"

"Ah jeez, it's complicated. I actually can't talk about most of it because it's still ongoing. They're trying to—" Claudia started to shiver. She pulled a thin sweater around her rail-thin body. It did get cold at night in the desert.

"Hey, Victor, can we go inside?" I asked.

"Nope. This is just a meet and greet and then a bye-bye and adios."

"We don't have much time. Tell me what happened to Ricky. What happened to you?" I asked.

"The cops held me for a long time, trying to get names of people who Ricky knew and who they could nail in a larger investigation. I'm going to have to testify against Ricky, and I bet you're going to as well. Ricky's in jail, and probably will be for a long time. The cops said if he testifies against some of the other gang members, he may get a reduced sentence."

I knew I would have to appear in court, it had been made clear from the start, but hearing it from Claudia made it real. Victor had been remarkably tight-lipped about it.

"I needed to see you one last time. We're pretty much breaking every rule by even meeting right now. At least you have Allie—she's family for you. Me? I've got no one."

"No. You've got me. Why can't you be part of my family?"

"Uh ... I don't know. You'd leave and come with me?"

"No, you could stay here," I said.

"Here? In this little town?"

"Yes. I think this is really the right place for Allie and me—a place to set down roots. Let's ask Victor."

"No. I'm sorry, I can't. Not here. I need a city."

"You need a city more than you need me?"

"Ah jeez, I don't know." She ran her hands through her short hair.

"'I don't know' is a pretty clear answer for me. See you later, sis." I turned to leave.

"Wait, don't go," Claudia pleaded.

I turned back to her.

"Allie and I are going to make it work here. I'd love for you to be here too, but I'm not going to force you. So, have a happy life." I hugged Claudia one last time, and walked away, not looking back. And that was the truth of the matter—there was no looking back.

I closed and locked the front door and dropped onto my sofa, shaking with anguish. Moments later, there was a knock at the door. I didn't answer.

"I'm leaving your computer and printer on the porch," Victor said through the door. "You'd best come and get them after I leave. You wouldn't want them to get stolen. Sorry about your sister. I shouldn't have brought her here."

I didn't respond. I sat on the sofa with tears streaming down my face.

TEN

Long before Allie got up for school, I sat on my couch, staring into my empty coffee cup. What the hell had happened last night? The unexpected and disappointing visit from Claudia had left me crushed. I wondered if I'd been too quick to shut down the notion of leaving Paradise. Maybe I should have had a conversation with Victor about what my other options would be. But somehow, that didn't feel right. For whatever reason, staying felt like the best decision. We'd had a rough start, possibly the worst introduction to a new town ever, but I hoped we could make it through this rough patch and create a fulfilling life here.

Our bumpy road to settling in reminded me of the paintings I used to create. When I'd apply those first few brush strokes to a canvas—and sometimes beyond that—I'd tell myself this piece was garbage. I thought it would never be good enough and was flawed beyond repair. But stubborn as I was, I would keep at it. Most people don't know that an artist doesn't sit down and paint the perfect picture in one sitting. It takes days, weeks, months. Slowly, slowly, the painting would improve, I could finally look at it and realize it was done, but more than that, it was beautiful.

That's what I wanted for Allie and me. While not a picture-perfect world, I wanted something we could look at and know was our best life. As crazy as it may seem, Paradise was my blank canvas, ready to become a masterpiece.

Claudia was gone. I would never see her again, at least as long as we were both in WITSEC. I had to wonder if we'd ever be able to leave the program, but I pushed aside that thought as being too depressing to even consider. Claudia and I didn't want the same things, and that was the crux of it.

Growing up, Claudia had always been the one to take the easy way out. Much more popular than me, she would skip her homework to hang out with friends. Teachers were willing to look the other way when she took advantage of a situation. Perhaps because she was pretty or more inclined to say the right things to be let off the hook. Me? I didn't play well with others and spent most of my free time with a sketch pad rather than hanging out with friends. Claudia and I always had different goals, and I would have to learn to live with that.

Once Allie was up, dressed, and had eaten breakfast, we walked to school with Boomer leading the way. It felt right to do something *usual* since we'd spent so much time recently dealing with such unusual circumstances.

After dropping Allie at school, Boomer and I headed down the hill toward the café. The Haunted History Tours office was open, and being currently unemployed, again, I went inside to see Derek Stramtussle about a job. I was concerned about how he'd react to me, given the suspicions that continued to swirl about his mother's untimely death. After all, he had told Darla Cotton that he'd seen someone lurking around his mother's property the night she died, and I was the only one in the area without an alibi.

The old clapboard building must have been a saloon in a past life. I tied Boomer's leash to the hitching post outside—originally meant for horses, not dogs, but it worked for us. I pushed through a set of swinging double-doors like I'd seen in old Western movies. Derek Stramtussle, wearing suspenders, black pants, a white pleated shirt with a bow tie, and a black bowler hat stood behind an old-timey bar. He clearly was dressed up to make an impression on tourists and potential customers. My first impression of Derek Stramtussle was that he was a little too slick—like a timeshare salesman. Like his sister, he was blond and blue-eyed and a few years younger than me. I couldn't put my finger on it, but there was something untrustworthy about him.

"Hello there," the man said, with a sickly-sweet smile. "Are you here for the two o'clock tour?"

"No, sorry. I'm actually here to see if you might be hiring. I'm Ruby Shaw," I said, reaching out for a handshake.

"Nice to meet you. I'm Derek Stramtussle. Are you new in town?" He removed his hat, gave the slightest bow, and took my hand—and oddly, didn't let go. "You're looking for a job?"

"Yes," I said, as confidently as I could.

"Actually, I'm always looking for people to add to my team. Though, I don't have any full-time work," he said. "You aren't living down on Castlerock by any chance, are you?"

"Yes. That's us," I said. I figured there was no reason to deny it since Derek would find out sooner or later.

"Ah yes, then I have heard about you. You live in one of my mother's houses," Derek said, his voice wobbling the tiniest bit.

"That's right. I'm so very sorry for your loss." I held my breath, hoping he wasn't going to accuse me of killing his mother.

"Thank you. Did you meet her? Or—"

"No, I'm sorry, I didn't. We'd only been in our new house for a few hours that night."

"Right, of course. Please, take a brochure, maybe you and your daughter can come on one of my tours someday."

This was interesting. I'd not mentioned Allie to him. I could see right through his act—he most certainly knew who I was.

"I don't think I can bring my daughter on the tour, do you?"

"It's not scary. It's mostly just a history tour."

"What I saw last Sunday night didn't seem like a history tour. A cloaked figure running around with an ax can't be historically accurate."

"We only do the reenactment tour the first weekend of October. I could see how that'd be inappropriate for your twelve-year-old daughter. But we recently cut that, and we're doing the whole tour in the downtown area, plus heading up to the Hilltop Hotel at the end of each tour for dessert."

Not only did he know about Allie, but he knew how old she was. There wasn't a single person in this town who didn't know about us. I'd put money on it.

"Just curious—how did you know about Allie?"

"Ah, news travels fast in this town, Ms. Shaw. Now, if you're interested in a job, I suggest you learn everything you can about our little town because if you become a tour guide, you're going to need to know the history of this place. Here's the tour's script. You'll want to memorize it, so you'll know what to say at each of the points of interest."

"Thanks. I won't let you down."

"And is there a Mr. Shaw?"

"No. There's not."

"You'll come to realize that the real men in this town are few and far between." He cracked a self-congratulatory smirk.

"Well, you must be one of them," I said as I turned on my heel and headed out the door.

Mentally, I beat myself up. I needed to work on keeping my mouth shut. It was challenging. I'd spent too long making sure everyone in my path knew I was a force to be reckoned with.

Now I needed to find a softer side. I hoped I hadn't blown it with Derek because a tour guide job sounded like a great option, other than the part about talking with a lot of people and having to tell stories about ghosts that were simply not true. But a job was a job, and I needed one desperately.

Arriving at Bette's Place, I found a post outside where I tied Boomer's leash while I went inside to get an iced tea for my walk home.

Bette bustled up to me at the door, and I placed my order with her.

Luke was in the kitchen, slinging eggs and hash browns, too busy to notice I'd arrived. I spotted Henry Villanueva seated alone in a corner booth. He waved me over to join him at his table.

"Hi, Mr. Villanueva. Nice to see you again," I said as I approached his table.

"Great to see you too. Please, call me Henry. Take a seat." He gestured to the seat across from him. "Good news—I have a job opening. That is, if you're still looking for work." I was pretty sure he'd added that last bit to cover for the fact that he, of course, knew I'd already lost my job at Ferrell's.

"That's wonderful. I'd love to hear more about it," I said. "I'm sorry I can't join you, but my dog is outside. I can't leave him there for long."

"It's the swing shift, our busiest time. You'd be getting people checked into their rooms. One o'clock until seven, Thursday through Sunday. The rest of the time, since we don't have that many guests coming and going, I can usually manage by myself."

"Sounds great."

"Call me when you're free, and perhaps you can come up for a tour and an interview."

"I'll call you to set something up as soon as possible."

I was going to have to find a babysitter for Allie, and fast. I knew she'd resist the idea of afterschool care, but there was no way I was going to leave her by herself until after dinner each night.

Bette brought my tea over as I headed for the door.

"Leaving so soon?" she asked. "Don't you want to stay and chat for a minute?" Questions, always questions from Bette.

"No, thanks. Boomer's outside, and I don't want to leave him for long. But maybe you can help me. Do you know where I could find a babysitter for Allie?"

"Does that mean things worked out for ya at Ferrell's Feed and Tack?" Bette asked, a note of surprise in her voice.

"No, actually. It turns out he wanted me for something less wholesome than ringing up purchases and carrying sacks of chicken feed."

"Darn. I was afraid of that. I should have warned ya about him," Bette said. "I'm sorry, sugar."

"The good news is, it looks like there might be an opening at the Hilltop Hotel. Swing shift. So I'll definitely need someone to help out with Allie after school."

"Ya sure Allie needs a babysitter? Your girl doesn't need one at her age," Bette said.

"She's not really used to being left alone."

"You'd both better catch up on some things; you can't be pampering her like that for the rest of her life, ya know," Bette said.

Bette didn't understand that in big cities, we were protective of our kids—some sort of perceived danger in a high-crime area —in a way that didn't seem to exist out in a middle-of-nowhere small town.

"I know, we're still getting used to things here. It's a little different from where we came from. So, do you know a sitter?"

"You could try Flora Lane, up the hill past the hardware store. She's kind of crazy, but maybe you'll like her."

"What? Is she crazy? Good crazy or bad crazy?"

"I guess you'll have to find out for yourself," Bette cackled as she grabbed a pot of coffee and made a beeline for an empty cup at the end of the counter.

Was Flora Lane crazy? Bette hadn't stuck around to tell me. I was going to have to find out. What I learned from many years of working in the art industry—and living in New York for that matter—was that crazy ranged from mildly eccentric to full-tilt insane. I was hoping Flora was the former.

I walked outside and was stunned to discover that Boomer was missing. His collar and leash were there, but there was no sign of him. I hoped he'd simply slipped out of his collar and run home. Allie would be devastated if Boomer was lost.

"Boomer! Come here, boy!" I shouted as I race-walked home, trying hard not to spill my tea. I crossed my fingers, hoping to find my dog by the front door, but no such luck. He hadn't gone home. Or had he? I recalled that his home, at least at some point in the past, had been right next door. I rushed to Mrs. Stramtussle's house, but he wasn't on the porch. The crime scene tape had been removed, and the door was ajar.

Did I dare enter? I was on a mission to find Boomer. That's what mattered most. This wasn't really trespassing, after all, I was simply looking for my dog.

"Boomer?" I called quietly as I entered. The living room looked unlived in—silent and cold. There was no sign of the dog. "Boooooomer," I called again, this time a little louder.

I crept from room to dusty room. In the kitchen, I found an open door leading down to a root cellar. Strange—my house, which had the same layout as this one, didn't have a root cellar like this. Just then, Boomer came dashing up the stairs and flew into my arms.

"Such a good boy," I whispered in the dog's soft ear. It was time to get out of there before anyone caught us. As I approached the front door, a figure filled its frame. I stopped in my tracks, holding Boomer tightly. Who had found us?

"What are you doing here?" His Texas twang gave him away.

"Victor! I could ask the same of you!"

"I came to check on you. I know you were pretty upset last night," Victor said.

"Let's get out of here."

"I'd say that's an excellent idea. I wouldn't want any local law enforcement to find you breaking and entering. You do know that if you're found guilty of a crime, we can toss you out of the WITSEC program."

"Yes, I know! I may have done the *entering* part, but I didn't do any *breaking*. The door was open. I was looking for my dog. Don't I get off the hook for that?"

"It's a damn good thing you found your dog, and that I located you before the sheriff's deputy did."

Back in my living room, Boomer settled into his dog bed. The little stinker had gotten me in trouble.

"I shouldn't have brought your sister by. I'm sorry about that," Victor said.

"I'm sorry too. I wish it had worked out. Thanks for bringing her. I'm crushed she didn't want to stay with us, but at least I know she's safe."

"She's safe as long as she doesn't make any silly moves."

"Right. I hear you loud and clear."

"Allie's at school—I take it that's going well?" Victor asked.

"Not great. The school wants to move her to a lower grade—which I am fighting. I've got to go to the school board to see if they'll retest her."

"Mm-hmm. Are you sure that's necessary?"

"I am. Allie could really use a win right now. I promise I won't do anything crazy."

"How are you holding up?"

"Me? I'm okay. Seems like every time I turn around, I run into a Stramtussle."

"And that's a problem?"

"It is if you want me to avoid the family of the lady who was murdered next door."

"Right. You staying out of her house would be a step in the right direction."

"I will, I promise. Under the radar, like you told me."

"I'd best be going." Victor said. "I left you a couple of lamps and some soil for that garden of yours. They're on the back porch. The lamps are officially from the marshals' office. The soil is from me."

I went to hug him, but he stood rigid, not returning my attempt at an embrace. So I clutched his forearm instead.

"Thank you, Victor. Really, truly."

After Victor left, I checked out what he brought me. A twenty-pound bag of potting soil rested against the railing on the back porch. For all of his complaining about my unusual requests, Victor had come through for me. I appreciated it more than he would ever know.

After pulling a beat-up table from the shed and dusting off the cobwebs, I shoved it to the end of the porch near the stairs. Then I hefted the bag of soil onto the table and filled the pots from the thrift shop. There was nothing more I could do until I got some plants. But it didn't matter, I was as happy as a pig in mud, or soil, as the case may be.

I brought the brass lamps with frosted glass shades inside and put them on the tables on each side of the sofa. Then I turned them on. Ahh. Glorious light. I spun in a circle to admire the room, which was looking better and better each day.

Boomer had settled into his dog bed and was chewing on something. It didn't look like a dog toy.

"What do you have there?" I asked the dog, crouching down to see what he had. "Come on, boy, let me see what you've got."

Boomer was reluctant to give up his goodie, but finally released it when I offered him his favorite frog-shaped squeaky toy.

I examined the piece of plastic. It was slender and red and had been thoroughly chewed, thanks to Boomer. It looked like the earpiece from a pair of eyeglasses—red glasses.

I called Darla.

"I found another clue."

"Great, is it going to implicate you in a crime? Because maybe you don't want to actively find ways of making yourself look even guiltier."

"No, I think this points to another suspect. I found—well, actually Boomer found—the temple from a pair of eyeglasses, and I'm pretty sure they belong to Mrs. Heard."

"Hm. Interesting. Where did you, or Boomer, find them?"

Rats! I hadn't thought this out. I couldn't tell her where I'd found them without telling her that I'd broken into Mrs. Stramtussle's house.

"Okay, I can explain. You see, Boomer wriggled out of his collar while I was at Bette's Place. I went looking for him and found him inside Mrs. Stramtussle's house. I guess it was his old home, so he wanted to go there, or was confused about where he lives now."

"Let me get this straight. You broke into the victim's house?"

"I didn't break in. The door was open. I was searching for my dog. He came home with the piece of plastic in his mouth. I only just discovered it. So strictly speaking, I found the temple to the glasses in my house."

"Which doesn't sound much better than you finding it at Mrs. Stramtussle's house."

She was right. I was sunk.

"How do you know the eyeglass temple is part of a pair of glasses owned by Mrs. Heard? Are you keeping track of everyone's eyewear?"

"Of course not. When Allie and I met with her on Monday she couldn't find her red glasses and asked Meg Stramtussle if she'd seen them. But then yesterday, she was wearing a different pair of glasses—silver. I don't think she ever found the red ones."

"Couldn't she have more than one pair of glasses?"

"Sure, but then how do we explain this thing that Boomer found?"

"I can't explain it. Do me a favor. Don't touch it—"

"Too late. Also, it's covered in dog slobber."

An audible sigh came from the receiver.

"Put it in a plastic bag, okay?"

"Will do, sir—er—I mean madam."

Silence.

"That was a joke. But listen, this piece of plastic means that Mrs. Heard was at Greta's house the night she died. Isn't it possible that Mrs. Heard is the killer?" I asked Darla.

"Those glasses could've belonged to Mrs. Heard," Darla grudgingly admitted. "It also could be that those were some old glasses that belonged to Greta Stramtussle. Maybe Boomer picked it up from the road or somebody placed at the scene of the crime to lead me on a wild goose chase."

"I thought you'd want to know. Believe it or not, I really am trying to help you."

"Well, thanks. But maybe you could try and stay out of trouble too." Darla sounded an awful lot like Victor. "Put the thing you found in a plastic bag, and I'll stop by the school to talk with Mrs. Heard."

"Can I ask for a favor?"

"You can ask, but I don't have to say yes, right?"

"Can you pick up Allie from school when you stop by to talk with the principal? After sprinting around looking for Boomer, I'm ready to take my sneakers off and have a beer."

"Sure, no problem. Maybe you should call the school office and let Meg know so there's no question about why I'm taking Allie home."

I called the school, but there was no answer. Where the heck was Meg?

ELEVEN

That evening, Allie and I walked to the bottom of our street for the Haunted Hayride. Allie tried to hide her excitement, but it was clear from her quick pace as we turned the corner onto Grimly Flats Road that she was looking forward to the event. She'd never been on a hayride, and I was pretty sure the only horses she'd seen in real life were ridden by police officers in Central Park.

We approached a gathering of people behind a large flatbed truck, all chatting in small groups. Bette greeted everyone with caramel apples as they arrived, and as she reached out to give Allie an apple, I saw a sparkle on the ring finger of her left hand. I'd never noticed a ring before, and this one wasn't easily overlooked. Allie pulled me away before I had a chance to ask Bette about it.

"Take my apple and find us a spot to sit. I'll go buy our tickets for the ride," I told Allie.

Derek Stramtussle stood beside a folding table with a display of tour brochures, collecting money for the event.

"Nice to see you this evening, Ruby," Derek said as I approached the table.

"Yes, you too," I said, handing him a ten-dollar bill.

"I've got some tours coming up soon, so I hope you've been practicing with your script."

"Yes, indeed," I lied. I hadn't even looked at it. I was glad to see that he wasn't holding a grudge after the smart aleck remark I'd made last time I saw him.

"Please, take a seat. We'll get the ride underway shortly."

Allie was sitting on the edge of the flatbed trailer, her feet dangling off the side. I squeezed in next to her, and she passed me my caramel apple. We each bit into them—they were absolutely delicious and incredibly messy. Juice ran down our hands.

"I thought this was going to be a horse-drawn carriage or something," Allie said between bites.

"Me too, but I guess this is the modern version," I said, passing Allie a napkin. She continued to munch on her apple, eyeing a few children her age who were admiring the horses. The horses, apparently, were for show and wouldn't be doing any actual pulling of the flatbed. "Do you know any of those kids?"

Allie shrugged. She was in one of her less-talkative moods. That was okay. She needed time. She'd entered that age when it became more awkward to simply approach another child and ask to be friends. Middle school was the worst. I remembered how it was when Claudia and I were growing up. She was always popular and had no trouble making friends. Me? I was more like Allie and had trouble fitting in.

"So, how is school?" I asked. I'd frankly been nervous to ask for fear I'd hear how much she hated it and how miserable she was having been moved down a grade.

"They're moving me to sixth grade next week." Her voice was flat as she looked straight ahead, not willing to look at me. Her excitement about the hayride suddenly faded. Rats! I should have waited to ask that question.

"I know, sweetheart, I'm trying to fix it. I hope you're not too miserable."

"Some of the kids aren't being too nice about it. Teasing me and saying I got rejected from seventh grade. It sucks, Mom. Everything about this place sucks."

"Not everything. This is fun, right?"

"Whatever, Mom. I just wish I had someone to eat lunch with."

As people found their seats, Derek Stramtussle climbed on a bale of hay and spoke to the crowd.

"Welcome, everyone, to the Haunted Hayride! We're happy to start this new tradition, which, of course, we're hoping will become a big tourist draw in the years to come."

There was a brief smattering of applause from the crowd, and Derek continued, "Now, as we go on this trip, we're going to see some spooky scenes, but don't worry, none are too gory and, of course, remember none of this is real. *Or is it?*" Derek let out a fake evil laugh, which was hilarious, and prompted a round of applause. He was trying to excite the audience and was finally having some success.

"Hi, sugar," Bette said, squeezing into a space—more like half a space—next to me. I saw the glint on her left ring finger again as she adjusted her purse in her lap. Could it be possible that Bette was engaged?

"Is that an engagement ring?" I asked.

"As a matter of fact, it is. Derek popped the question last night!" Bette wiggled the fingers of her left hand in front of my face. It was a lovely ring, with a large diamond featured prominently among swirls of yellow gold on a broad band. I wondered where Derek got it. I hoped he'd bought it and hadn't yanked it from his mother's cold hand after he'd found her murdered—or worse, after he'd murdered her. Could Derek be the culprit? It seemed impossible that he would have been so brazen as to kill his mother, steal her wedding ring, and turn around days later to give it to his betrothed. I couldn't imagine he was the killer, though if he were guilty, it sure would take the heat off of me.

"Congratulations," I gulped. It all seemed more than a little strange to me. I didn't think Derek was much of a catch, but I supposed that options for marriage material were thin on the ground in a small town.

A tractor hitched to the front of the flatbed rumbled to life and slowly pulled the cart along Grimly Flats. Horses flanked each side of the flatbed, adding an air of excitement to the event. We passed Luke's farm on the far side of the street. There were lights on in the little house past some vegetable beds and shade structures. Since I didn't see him on the hayride, I assumed he'd decided to skip the event. I hadn't realized it, but I'd hoped I might see him tonight.

The first spooky scene we came to was a dummy hanging from a tree. The artist in me couldn't help noticing the proportions of the figure weren't quite right—the head was a little too big, the arms a little too long.

Bette nudged me with her elbow.

"Pretty good, right? That's the one I made."

I nodded and made positive-sounding noises. It was the best I could do.

After that was a delightful collection of pumpkins painted to look like all sorts of funny monster faces. Not terribly scary, but pretty darn cute and all painted by the kindergarteners at the Paradise School.

Next, we came to a scene that was much gorier than I expected. A woman was lying prone across a bale of hay. On her back were four red piercings in a line across her blouse. A bloody pitchfork lay on the ground. It looked far too realistic to have been the work of some amateur artist. My head started to spin. I grabbed hold of Allie and covered her eyes. I had a horrible feeling about this.

A rumble ran through the crowd. Then a woman walking beside the truck shouted, "That's not a dummy! Oh my God—it's Mrs. Heard!"

The tractor came to a screeching halt, and the man driving it yelled something unintelligible as he climbed down from his perch to get a closer look. There was a simultaneous gasp as we all came to the same horrifying conclusion. Mrs. Heard had been murdered. While some people craned their necks to get a glimpse of this horrid sight, many others looked away in shock.

Derek Stramtussle came trotting up from behind the flatbed and tried to take control of the situation.

"Everyone needs to get back! Let me through!" The crowd parted, and Derek stepped forward to the body. He stumbled a little when he saw the murder scene—a real murder scene, not a staged spectacle from one of his tours.

"Okay, everyone, there's nothing to see here. Why don't you all walk back up to where we started. There's free hot apple cider for everyone." Under his breath, he said something urgent and panicky to Bette, who had climbed off the flatbed and was dialing a number on her cell phone.

"Come on, Allie, time to go," I said, grabbing her by the hand and pulling her through the chaotic mass of people who were scrambling off the trailer, finding their loved ones, and crying in grief. My heart pounded as we hustled by everyone and rushed away from the scene, retracing our steps on Grimly Flats and Castlerock Road.

Finally, Allie spoke.

"Was that really Mrs. Heard? What do you think happened to her?"

"I don't know. I honestly don't. But I'm certain we don't need to be there for all that horrible stuff."

TWELVE

There was a killer among us. Was it safe to continue living in Paradise? I didn't want to leave, but it certainly looked like we'd gone from one dangerous situation to another. While I had promised Victor (and myself) that I wouldn't meddle in a murder investigation, that was no longer possible, especially now that two women were dead.

How were Mrs. Stramtussle and Mrs. Heard connected? More importantly, who would want to harm both of them? I had to assume that there was only one killer, but it was certainly possible there were two killers on the loose. That was hard to imagine, but so was finding out my brother-in-law was mixed up with the Mexican Mafia.

Boomer had found the temple from what had to have been Mrs. Heard's glasses in the house next door. So, Mrs. Heard was in Greta Stramtussle's house the night Greta was killed, there was no doubt in my mind about that. Up until last night, Mrs. Heard was the only suspect, and now she was dead. I had a bad feeling that placed me back in the number-one-suspect position, and I didn't like it there one bit.

I went to the kitchen and started the coffee maker so it

would be ready when I got out of the shower. There was nothing like a cool shower on a hot day to refresh me. I toweled off and dressed in my standard jeans and T-shirt. On my way to the kitchen, there was a knock at the door.

A quick look through the peephole confirmed my suspicions about who would be visiting me at such an early hour on a Saturday morning. It was Darla, and it was clear this wasn't a social visit. My first clue was that she was wearing her tan sheriff's uniform, complete with reflective aviator glasses. I opened the door, plastering on a pleasant smile.

"Sorry to bother you," Darla said, not a drop of emotion in her voice. She stood in the doorway, getting out her spiral notebook and pen. "I need to interview everyone at the hayride last night, and I have several witnesses who told me you were there but departed abruptly."

"Yes, sorry, I left. I didn't want Allie to be exposed to all that ugliness. She's a sensitive girl," I said.

"Right, I got that," Darla said, scribbling some notes. "But here's the thing, you doing something suspicious like making a quick getaway means everyone is looking at you sideways. It looks like you've got something to hide."

She didn't know the half of it.

"It was my protective maternal instinct kicking in—I didn't want to upset Allie," I said as I pressed my fingers to my temples. Last night had been rough. I'd been unable to sleep without being interrupted by thoughts of Mrs. Heard, wondering if we'd landed in the wrong town and if it was time to get out of here. "Besides, I was on the flatbed the whole time. Bette was sitting right next to me—I have an alibi."

"It's pretty clear that Mrs. Heard was killed before—not during—the event. She'd been down at the hayride site setting up the pumpkins for the kindergarten class. When I stopped at the school to talk with Mrs. Heard about her glasses yesterday, she wasn't there and neither was Meg."

"That means someone down at the hayride site must've done it. Derek and Bette were both setting up, I'm sure."

"Right, and they both can vouch they were together the whole time."

"So, you think I just walked down the street in broad daylight, killed this woman, and then strolled home?"

"It's one theory."

"Who would want to harm Mrs. Heard?" I asked. "She seemed like a nice person when I met her."

"And when was that?" Darla still hadn't come inside. Instead, she loomed in my doorway, but she had finally taken her sunglasses off.

"The last time I saw her was the day before yesterday. We didn't have the best interaction, sort of a disagreement." I stopped talking. This wasn't good. Not good at all. "Now ... come on in, I was just brewing some coffee. I could make it iced and even put it in a travel mug for you. You must be hot in that uniform."

"And what did you discuss with Mrs. Heard?" Darla asked, refusing to be distracted.

"We discussed Allie's placement at school. She was dropped a grade lower than she should be, and well, Mrs. Heard and I didn't quite see eye to eye on that. Seriously, it's not a reason to murder someone with a pitchfork, or with any other sort of garden tool for that matter." I tried once again to usher Darla in. She didn't budge.

"We ran some quick prints on the pitchfork and guess whose prints are on it?"

I had a bad feeling about this.

"Let me guess, mine and Luke's. Was there still a price tag from Ferrell's Feed and Tack on it?"

"There was not. But dang, Ruby, how am I supposed to assume you're innocent?"

"Because you know I have no reason to kill anyone in this

town."

"Might you be able to explain why the murder weapon had your fingerprints on it?"

"Because I was working at Ferrell's Feed and sold a pitchfork to Luke."

"And how do you suppose that pitchfork ended up skewering Mrs. Heard's back?"

"No idea. Well, maybe I do. Luke's farm is across the street from the hayride site. I'd hate to think Luke was the culprit. Why don't I talk with him and see if I can find out where he was in the hours leading up to the hayride."

Not wanting to throw Luke under the bus, I added, "But just because it was his pitchfork doesn't mean he killed Mrs. Heard. Anyone could have taken it from the back of his truck or gotten it from his property across the street from where she was murdered, right? Besides, what reason could Luke possibly have for killing Mrs. Heard?"

"You've made some good points." Darla's voice softened a bit.

"I mean, if Luke has no history with Mrs. Heard, then he's got no motive for killing her, right?" It made sense to me, though it meant we'd have to keep looking for a suspect. "I almost forgot. Mrs. Heard's glasses." I grabbed the plastic bag from the coffee table and handed it over to her. "Sorry for the dog slobber."

Darla held up the bag and looked at the piece of red plastic. "It sure does look like part of an eyeglass frame."

"That's what I thought too. Now, will you please come in? I can show you what I've done to get my pots ready for planting. I think I need some cactus seeds. Do you know where I can buy some?"

"Sorry, I've got to go track down some other people who were at the hayride," Darla said as she turned to go. I started to shut the door behind her, but she stopped the door with her hand and poked her head back in.

"By the way, forget about cactus seeds. You've got to get some cuttings." She'd put her sunglasses back on, so I wouldn't see her eye roll.

Allie was playing with Boomer in the backyard, such as it was. They'd recently made up a game in which Allie rolled a ball down the hill and Boomer would run after it and catch it before it got lost in the sagebrush at the bottom of the yard. Unfortunately, Allie had yet to figure out how to get Boomer to bring the ball back to her once he'd found it. This resulted in her having to hike down the hill and back up every few minutes.

There was a knock at the front door, and I ran to get it. It was Luke, standing on my front porch with a tub of wilted veggies, looking as handsome as ever.

"Wow! I had no idea you'd be coming up with scraps for my compost pile so soon. Thank you so much. Let me show you where to put them."

"I've got more in my truck, ma'am."

"Will you cut it out with the *ma'am* business? Just Ruby, okay?"

"I can't say no to a lady," Luke said, looking straight at me with those sultry denim-blue eyes. I thought I was going to melt right there on the spot. It wasn't the sizzling Arizona sun that overheated me but the hot man standing before me. I couldn't lie to myself; I was attracted to Luke.

I took him around the side yard, down the stairs, and onto the porch behind the house while Allie and Boomer worked on variations of the fetch game that didn't require Allie to run after the ball more than Boomer did. Luke stopped for a moment and watched.

"Seems like those two are meant for each other," he said nodding toward Allie and Boomer.

"It seems like it."

"Is your daughter doing okay?"

"As well as can be expected. Things will settle down soon, I'm sure."

Luke gave me a little nod of agreement.

"Now, where do you want this compost pile?"

"Let's put it right there." I pointed to a corner at the edge of the terrace. Right now it was a plot of gravel and sand, but someday I hoped it would be a lush garden. "That way it's pretty close to the storage area under the house, where I thought I could keep some of my tools and supplies."

"Let's take a look at what you've got," Luke said, opening the shed's door. Other than a pile of tarps and a crate of old bottles, it was empty. "Not much to speak of. You'll want to get yourself a pitchfork so you can turn your compost. I'd loan you my new one, but it seems someone must've stolen it from my truck."

"Luke? Do you know what happened last night?"

"No, can't say that I do. I pretty much like to stay at home on the weekends. Friday night I usually find a good movie on TV, and Peaches and I curl up and watch a show. I make dinner with some of what I grow on the farm. It's quiet, the way I like it."

I filled Luke in on what happened during the hayride and told him the weapon that had been used to kill Mrs. Heard was the pitchfork I'd sold him at Ferrell's. Luke was possibly the calmest man I'd ever met. He took all of the news in stride.

"It seems to me someone must've taken the pitchfork out of the back of my truck while it was parked at my house. I'll just have to explain to the sheriff's department that's what happened. I didn't know the woman who died, did you?"

His question made me realize something important—Luke must have been an outsider like me. If he'd lived in Paradise for years, he'd have known the school principal.

"I'd met her a couple of times. She seemed nice. We had an argument, but it was no big deal. I'm sure the sheriff's department will get it sorted out."

"Let's go get the rest of your scraps," Luke said.

As we hiked back up the stairs to Luke's truck, I wondered about Peaches. It couldn't be a woman's name, so I assumed it was a pet, which seemed like a safe topic.

"Who's Peaches? Your dog?"

"No, ma'am—"

"Ruby."

"No, she's my cat. She was a stray I adopted from Greta's animal rescue. If Greta had her way, I'd have an entire clowder of cats—"

"Wait, what? A clowder?"

"That's a herd of cats. I thought everyone knew that." He quirked a smile. "I told Greta I only needed one. I got Peaches hoping she'd be a good mouser, but she prefers a catnip toy and a warm lap."

"What a slacker!" I said with a laugh. In my mind's eye, I imagined this rugged man with a cat in his lap. The image made him all the more appealing. Luke laughed along with me and agreed that Peaches had been a disappointing hunter but a good companion.

We grabbed a double-handled tub from his truck and carried it down the steps together before dumping it. After a few more trips, we'd put all the veggies in a big pile so they could start their decomposition, and in a matter of months, I'd have glorious compost—a key ingredient in any successful garden. I pulled out a tarp from the shed and threw it over the green heap.

"That should start breaking down really fast in this heat," Luke said as we headed back up the path. We both were a little sweaty from the trips up and back to his truck, even this early in the day.

"Would you like to come in for a glass of water?" I asked.

"No, thank you, Ruby," Luke said, finally getting my name right.

"Thanks for bringing the scraps down."

"No problem whatsoever. I'll bring more when I have them. I almost forgot. I brought you a little present." Luke pulled a canvas bag from the back of his truck and handed it to me. It was about the size and shape of a basketball. I couldn't imagine what it was. "Go on, look inside."

Opening the bag, I discovered a giant ball-shaped cactus.

"Um…"

"It's a barrel cactus," Luke said, with a hopeful glance at me. "I thought you needed something to grow if you were starting a garden."

"Thank you! It's wonderful. Really. What am I supposed to do with it? Stick it in the ground?"

"I sliced it off one of the specimens down at my place, so you need to let it sit out for a while. You can't plant it until there's a callus over the cut or else it'll rot."

"It won't die in the meantime?"

"Cacti are pretty hardy. You'll have to come down to my farm someday, I can show you what I grow. More than just cacti; I've got succulents, vegetables, and ornamental plants that I sell at local nurseries. It helps me pay the bills, and I get a lot of enjoyment out of it too."

After Luke had gone, I found Allie in her room, setting up our new computer.

"How's it going, sweetheart?"

"Pretty good. I found a game on the computer," Allie said, not looking up from what looked like some sort of Tetris brick-building game.

"Did you get us on the internet too?" I asked.

"Yep, pretty easy." Allie refocused on the multicolored bricks dropping from the top of the screen. She finished her game and turned to me.

"Mom? Have you ever thought about going on a date?"

"Yes. I have. I have been on dates, many times." I held up the canvas bag Luke had given me. "Come check out what Luke gave me."

"You've been on dates since I was born?" Allie clearly wasn't dropping the topic. She followed me down to the potting table behind the house.

"Yes, as a matter of fact. I went on dates and left you with a babysitter when you were little."

"Oh."

"Do you have something you want to ask me?"

"It's about Luke. He's really nice," Allie said.

"He *is* nice, but not really my type. Plus, I have a lot on my plate right now, and ..."

"So, you don't like him?"

"I didn't say that—"

"Oh, so you *do* like him," she said, a big grin on her face.

"I didn't say that, either. Right now, my focus is on you and me and getting our new lives set up here in Paradise." I didn't tell Allie that I needed to find a murderer so that everyone in town would stop considering me their number one suspect.

I gently rolled the barrel cactus out of the bag and into an empty terra-cotta planter on the potting bench, being careful not to touch it.

"Ta-dah!" I said, admiring my spiny new prize.

"Mom? Did Luke give you a cactus?"

"Yes, he did."

"That's pretty weird," Allie said, tentatively touching one of the spines on the rib of the plant. "Sharp!"

"It's probably best if you leave this alone. I know it looks dangerous, but it's beautiful too. The colors, the repetition of the ribs running from top to bottom, and the perfectly symmetrical spines." I had gone into artist mode, studying this object as a work of art. I had to admit, I was fascinated.

"And why can't your new life have a boyfriend in it?" Allie persisted.

I sighed.

"Allie Shaw—what a little matchmaker! Listen, I know you want me to be happy, and maybe someday a boyfriend will make sense. But for now, no. I'm figuring out who the new me is and working to be the best mom I can be for you."

"You're a great mom," Allie said. "You don't need to work on it."

* * *

LONG AFTER ALLIE had gone to bed, I thought about Luke. He was quite attractive and kind and seemed to have a sense of humor. The man gave me a cactus and had a cat named Peaches. But mostly what I thought about was whether Luke could have killed Mrs. Heard. His house was across the road from where she died, and she had been killed with his pitchfork. But he didn't seem to know her. In fact, other than Bette, it didn't seem like Luke knew anyone in town. I wondered if he knew Mrs. Stramtussle. Perhaps she owned not only the properties on Castlerock but also those on Grimly Flats. I was unsure how to find that out, though I might simply be able to ask one of Mrs. Stramtussle's kids. One thing was certain, if Luke was by himself the night Mrs. Heard died, with only his cat to vouch for him, he was another suspect without an alibi.

THIRTEEN

Now that I had a lead on a job opportunity at the hotel, I needed a babysitter for Allie. Bette had told me I'd find Flora Lane's shop beyond the hardware store. So, after dropping off Allie at school, I took a stroll through town, doing a little window shopping to see if I could find her store.

Just past Hardware Heaven was a narrow alley paved with multicolored stepping stones leading to a small shop in a shady alcove. On the door was a little sign in perfect calligraphy. *Flora Lane*.

I had no idea what she'd be like, not sure which version of crazy Bette was talking about. I wanted to find out for myself, and I could decide whether I should even mention babysitting to Flora.

The shop was dark and intimate and packed with unique— make that bizarre—items on every shelf, nook, and cranny. No one appeared to be there—no customers or a proprietor anywhere to be found.

"Hello?" I called, looking around for signs of life. With a couple of recent murders, I suddenly had the morbid thought that I hoped I wasn't about to discover another body. "Hello?"

A woman with frizzy white hair and enormous goggles leaped up from behind the counter. I jumped back, more startled than afraid.

"Aha! Found it!" She held something small in a pair of tweezers. "Well, hello there!" the woman said, speaking louder than necessary in the tiny space.

"What'd you find?" I asked, peering at what she held but also wary given her erratic behavior.

"A diamond. I dropped it on the floor. They're slippery little buggers."

"I can imagine," I said, stepping closer and trying to assess the situation. Was she crazy or just eccentric? Eccentric I could handle; insane, not so much. I wasn't even sure this was Flora Lane.

"Now, what can I do for you?" the woman asked, placing the gem in a tiny glass dish out of harm's way.

"I was looking for Flora Lane."

"You're in luck. You found her! Nice to meet you. And you are?"

"Ruby Shaw," I extended my right hand to shake.

"Ruby, now that's a pretty name. Goes with a pretty stone, like that ring you've got." Flora still had her goggles on, which magnified her eyes to unnatural proportions. She wiped her hands on the front of her purple overalls and pulled my hand in close to take a good look at my ring.

This ring was special to me. My grandmother had given it to my mother when she was pregnant with me. When my mother gave the ring to me at age twenty, she told me the ring had come from Taxco, a famous silver mining town in Mexico where my grandparents lived before immigrating on the US. Inspired by the ring, I chose the name Ruby the day I entered witness protection so that I would not only be connected to my mother and grandmother but to my family's Mexican heritage.

"Thanks," I said, "and nice goggles you've got there."

"Oh! Sorry. I forgot I had them on." Flora pushed her goggles up to the top of her head, creating a makeshift headband to contain the pile of platinum hair sticking out in all directions. She plopped onto a stool behind the counter. "Now, how can I help you?"

"I'm new in town—"

"I figured as much, given that I've never met you," she raised a white eyebrow and gave me a long, hard look. Then she tugged on the white cords next to each ear, popping out a set of earbuds. "I like to listen to some good marching band music while I'm working—keeps me energized, if you know what I mean. You know Sousa? *Bum-bum-bum BAH da, bum-bum-bum DUH dahhh.*" Had she not been sitting, I'm sure she would have started marching.

I didn't know what she meant, but I was glad she'd removed her headphones. She was talking at a much more reasonable volume now.

"I heard from Bette Taylor that you might be available for some afternoon and evening babysitting."

"Perhaps. I could use a little extra cash, sales haven't been so good lately."

"I've heard that from a lot of business people around town. Not enough tourists coming through."

"True, but there's not much we can do about it."

"There's not?"

"No, no, no. Of course not. Haven't you seen those switch-backs? You can't get a bus up here. It would be a nightmare."

"People could drive their cars up, right?"

"Then we'd need scads of parking lots for all those vehicles," Flora said. "Now, lots of folks in town, they'd be keen to have tour buses parking down there on Castlerock Road."

"That's where my house is."

"Ah, so you're the one who's living in number thirty-three."

"Yes, my daughter and I."

"You wouldn't want busses clogging up your street, right?"

"No, of course not."

"So, you see my point. Tourists—you can't kill 'em."

That wasn't what I expected the summation of the debate about tourism in Paradise would be. Perhaps Claudia was right —a big city would have been better, at least I'd have a modicum of anonymity, and I could simply walk past the crazy people. There was a long pause in our conversation. If I left quickly, perhaps Flora would forget I mentioned babysitting.

"Now, you asked about babysitting?"

Rats! She hadn't forgotten.

"My daughter needs an afternoon babysitter. I've got an employment opportunity at the Hilltop Hotel, but unless I find someone to watch her, I can't take the job—and I really need the job."

"How old is this daughter of yours?"

"Twelve."

"She could certainly be at home by herself, couldn't she?"

"She's not used to being left alone, and I think I'd be happier if she had someone with her until I got home at seven."

"Golly, that is an awfully long time for her to be home by herself, especially if she's never done it before."

"So, you'll do it?" I asked, hopeful something would finally go my way in this town. And hopeful, as well, that I hadn't just hired a crazy woman to babysit my daughter after school.

"Sure, we can give it a try."

"Great. I'll let you know my start date and we can work out payment. So, you know my address."

"I can't come to your house. I've got a shop to run. Your daughter will have to come here after school."

"Hmm. That's not really—"

"I can't close up early. What if a customer came by?" That seemed unlikely. I was ready to give up, but I needed the hotel job, so I really had to get a babysitter.

"You want to babysit my daughter *here* after school?"

"Sure. She'll be wild about it, I promise," Flora said, spinning in a circle to admire all the crazy gimcracks lining the shelves.

I forced a smile. "Okay, I'll be in touch," I said, closing the door behind me. I wasn't sure if choosing Flora Lane was a good idea or not, but we'd know soon enough.

As I stepped into the narrow alley, a small nut-brown cat skittered by me. He had to be one of the last few feral cats in town, thanks to Greta Stramtussle's work on reducing their population.

Was it possible her demise had something to do with the work she'd done with animals? I recalled what Allie told me about Greta having killed all the wild cats. Clearly, that wasn't entirely true, since there were a few I'd spotted in my travels through town.

Darla told me there was a vet who had an office in town. I wondered what he knew about the feral cats and if he had any information on what had happened to them. Fortunately, I had a brand-new dog who would need a vet someday. I even knew who he'd belonged to before he came into our care.

A few doors down from the thrift shop I found Sweet's Pet Clinic. The vet greeted me as I entered his office.

"Hi, I'm Ruby Shaw. I adopted Greta Stramtussle's dog," I said.

"Dr. Dan Sweet. Nice to meet you. Most people just call me Dr. Dan. So, you adopted Ricky, I heard about that." Of course, he had. Dr. Dan, with his dark hair, hazel eyes, and perfect tan, along with this white lab coat, made him look like a leading man right out of central casting. Definitely not my type, but I could see how other women might find his perfection attractive.

"We like to call him Boomer. Anyway, the reason I came in was I wanted to make sure his shots were up to date." This was the best excuse I had for being there. It was my hope that I might be able to chat him up about the feral cats while he looked up Boomer's records.

"Let's see here," the vet said, pulling out a file folder that must've contained records for the dog formerly known as Ricky. "Looks like he's all up to date. Not surprising—Greta liked to keep on top of the immunizations for her animals."

"Animals? Did she have more than her dog?"

"Only if you count all the cats in town," Dr. Dan said. "Of course, I'm not sure you can count them. They never really belonged to anyone—feral—and not adoptable, poor things."

"I'd heard she was able to control the feral cat population. That doesn't mean she—"

"Does it mean she euthanized a bunch of cats? No, of course not," he said. "Now, I wasn't here at the time. My father, Dan Sr., spayed and neutered a lot of them. Greta would trap the cats, and bring them in—dozens!"

"I'm glad to hear they weren't just put to death."

"Oh, Greta wouldn't have stood for that. My dad would sterilize all the cats she brought him. She placed the adoptable kittens in homes through her nonprofit animal rescue. If they weren't adoptable, my father would clip an ear so we knew they'd been fixed and put them back in town. This all started about six years ago. Most of the wild kitties have died off, but you'll see some around town."

"Thanks for filling me in on what your dad and Greta did. It seems their work really turned things around for the community."

"Yeah, they were quite a team."

"A couple?"

"No, just friends."

"Your father must've been upset when Greta died," I said.

"He's been pretty broken up about it. That, along with Meg and I getting divorced, it's been a pretty bad year."

"Oh, wow. That has got to be hard." Aha! Meg and Dr. Dan

had been married. Slowly I was figuring out all the connections in this town.

"It's all pretty complicated," the vet said, crossing out the name Ricky and writing Boomer on the folder before closing it. "You should bring Boomer back in six months for his rabies shot." It was clear that was all the information I was going to get from him.

After such an enlightening conversation with the vet, I swung over to school to pick up Allie.

The school bell rang, and the students poured from the classrooms. Allie was at the back of a pack of girls, and I could tell her mood was as dark as ever as she charged past me.

"Hey, wait for me," I said, trying to catch up, which was futile. Allie kept walking, just out of my reach. When we finally got home, she went straight to her room, slamming the door behind her. I decided to give her some time to cool down before checking on her.

I grabbed a beer and a bag of chips and sat down on the steps outside the kitchen, looking down at the dismal yard below. I imagined what it could be like once I got going with planting. It was going to take time and energy, but I had plenty of both. Boomer came out and sat beside me, looking up expectantly as I took a chip from the sack and ate it. His eyes followed my hand as it traveled from the bag to my mouth.

"Oh, all right. Here's one for you."

I tossed a chip half-way down the staircase. Boomer raced down the steps, gobbled the chip, and ran back up to wait for another.

"Sorry, you're on a strict one-chip-a-day diet." I gave him a pat on the head, and he trotted inside. I followed him since I knew that I'd need to deal with Allie and her latest mood sooner or later. I grabbed an ice cream sandwich from the freezer for her. Perhaps that might tempt her to open up. I tapped on her bedroom door.

"Allie, can I come in? I have ice cream."

"Yeah," came a muffled answer.

I opened the door slowly, quietly, not wanting to alarm Allie and send her into another sullen silence.

"Baby—"

"Do *not* call me that." She looked at me darkly from across the room, curled up on her bed.

"Why not?"

"I'm not a baby anymore."

"Okay, sweetheart—I can still call you sweetheart, right?"

"Yeah. That's okay."

"I have some news for you. I may have found a job, so I don't think I'm going to be able to pick you up after school anymore."

"What?" Allie sat straight up, her mouth gaping.

"I'm sorry, I know it's a challenge."

"No, it's not! It's normal. You want to know why I'm upset? Everyone's teasing me, calling me a baby. Even you. And you know why? Because my *mommy* has to drop me off and pick me up from school every day."

This was news to me. I had no idea that walking Allie to and from school was causing her problems. It wasn't going to go over well when I told her that I'd found a babysitter for her—a *baby*sitter.

"I thought you wanted me to walk you to school. That was one of the things we could do here that would be like when we were in New York."

"It's not like that here. The only kids whose moms drop them off and pick them up from school are the kindergarteners."

"You're *not* upset that I can't pick you up from school?"

"No! I'm relieved. I just didn't know how to tell you."

I was pleased to hear Allie tell me the truth and share what was happening in her life with me. I sat down on the bed next to her, wrapped my arms around her, and held her tight.

"You won't have me bothering you anymore on the way to school in the morning. I hope that helps."

"It totally does! It's okay for me to walk home by myself too?" Allie asked, her expression brightening.

"With this new job I won't get home until after seven most nights. So, I found you a … uh … a person for you to hang out with after school since I can't be here. A kid-sitter." This was a lame name for a babysitter, but it was the best I could do.

Allie rolled her eyes. "A babysitter? Seriously? Ma-ahm!"

I hated it when *mom* became a two-syllable word.

"You'll be walking over to Flora Lane's. It's an interesting place. I think it might remind you of some of my friends' art studios—full of all sorts of crazy stuff."

"Like what kind of stuff?" I'd clearly piqued her interest. She took the ice-cream sandwich from me and peeled back the wrapper.

"A little bit of everything. Antiques, pottery, taxidermy, welded sculptures, jewelry, and vintage things of all sorts. Flora's got a lot going on."

"You're leaving me at a junk shop. And where will you be?"

"If all goes well, I'll be working at the Hilltop Hotel. So, you'll go to Flora's shop, and then once the shop closes, she'll bring you home or I'll pick you up on my way home from work."

Allie grumbled, but not too much. I'm sure the ice cream helped her mood. I knew it always helped mine.

FOURTEEN

"Okay, Mom," Allie said, tying the shoelaces on her Converse sneakers. This would be her first morning walking to school by herself.

"Are you sure you know how to get there?"

"There's only one main road. As long as I head uphill, I'll get there." She rolled her eyes.

"Because the day we found Boomer you headed the wrong direction and—"

"I was upset then. I promise it'll be fine. You know, if you let me have a cell phone, I could call you once I got to school and tell you I had gotten there safely."

That child of mine! Give her an inch, and she'll take a mile.

"Oh, no. We have already talked about that. No way."

She shrugged and put on her backpack, knowing she'd lost the phone battle but had won the walking-to-school battle.

"Bye, Mom," Allie said as she inched toward the open door, ready to escape in case I changed my mind.

"I'll pick you up after school so we can go to Flora Lane's, okay?"

"Okay." She gave me a quick nod, then turned and trotted down the steps without looking back.

"Don't talk to strangers!" I shouted after her. How had I become such a worrywart? Because there really were evil people in the world, and I'd come just a little too close to one of them.

I needed to watch her go, just to follow a little way. I slid on my shoes and crept down the steps as stealthily as possible. I looked up the street. She was gone, already out of sight. I hiked up the sidewalk, but she was nowhere to be found. She must've really been moving fast.

Just then, Allie jumped out from behind the trash cans in front of me.

"Boo!"

"Aaahh! You scared me to death. You want to be an orphan? Keep scaring me like that, and I may die from a heart attack," I said pressing my palm on my chest.

"I was just joking around. I thought you might follow me. So predictable, Mom."

"I wanted to make sure you were safe. Okay, no more following you." I watched anxiously as Allie trudged up the hill to school without me. I knew there was no chance she'd get lost. We'd been to school and back for the last week, so she certainly knew the way. I did worry that there were bad guys out there, but I reassured myself that my *Overprotective New Yorker Mom Mode* was just dialed a little too high.

Back inside, I called Henry Villanueva.

"It's Ruby Shaw. Would this morning be a convenient time for me to come to the hotel?"

"That would be perfect. Since we had a few guests check out earlier, I'm not busy right now."

I regarded myself in the bathroom mirror. I was having one of those bad hair days when every single curl on my head had decided to go a different direction. I wrangled my hair into a ponytail to keep it out of the way and made sure the T-shirt I wore was clean. That was as good as it got for me most days.

Boomer could tell I was getting ready to leave, and he followed me to the door.

"Sorry, you stay here and guard the house."

He gave me that pathetic dog look that said *I know I'll never see you again* as I closed the door. I briefly considered bringing him with me. His pathetic expression seemed so authentic, but didn't think it was wise to bring a dog to a job interview.

The Hilltop Hotel was a boxy three-story building. I was no expert on architecture, but I was pretty sure it was Georgian, lacking the elaborate decorations of a Victorian building. According to the brochure Derek had given me at the Haunted History Tours office, the hotel was formerly a hospital, and was now inhabited by several ghosts. There were so many made-up stories, it was difficult to know what was actually the truth. While it was likely a hospital at some point in the past, it was unlikely that it was currently haunted.

When I arrived, Henry was stationed behind the reception desk with a young woman who must've been an employee. Henry wore a black blazer with a cravat, and his employee sported a matching black jacket with a floppy black bow around her neck. Noting the proper work attire for a haunted hotel, I realized I was underdressed in my sneakers, T-shirt, and capris.

"Hello there, Ms. Shaw. Thanks so much for coming," Henry said, reaching out to shake my hand.

"My pleasure. I'm looking forward to seeing your hotel," I replied.

"I thought I'd start with a tour, and while we do that, you can tell me a little bit about yourself. I can't guarantee we'll see any ghosts while you're here." Like Allie might have done, I rolled my eyes—internally, of course.

"That's okay, I'm not really sure I believe in ghosts."

"We've had a lot of people say that over the years, and trust me, by the time they leave, they're believers."

We started in the hotel lobby, which had an eclectic mix of vintage furniture and original Southwestern art on the walls. Spanning the lobby's length, several sofas were arranged so that when seated, guests could look out the expansive floor-to-ceiling windows at the valley below. Next to the lobby was a large parlor filled with wingback chairs situated in groupings. Interesting lamps and objets d'art were scattered around to give the spacious room an artful feel I appreciated. From this vantage point, the landscape's shades of red, gray, and green were stunning. I could look at the landscape for hours. On the far side of the parlor was a restaurant, most of which had been shut down, with only a few tables set up for cocktails and dessert.

Down a short hallway on the opposite side of reception was an old-fashioned elevator with embossed copper doors. A half-moon floor indicator with an embellished arrow and arc of numbers was installed above the doors.

"Now, over here is our haunted elevator," Henry said, guiding me to the end of the hallway. "As you know, Paradise exists because copper was found in these hills, and our little town was built for the miners. These doors are made from some of the last of the copper from the Copper King mine."

The doors were beautiful. I appreciated the intricate engraved design in the panels, but more than that, I appreciated Henry giving me some real, historical information about the town, rather than obviously fictional stories about hauntings.

"Frequently, late at night, the elevator goes up and down on its own. It carries within it the ghost of a late customer who once got his head caught in the door and was decapitated!" Henry continued. It was too good to be true that he'd skip the spooky—and likely fabricated—part of his spiel.

The elevator certainly didn't look haunted at the moment,

and it seemed highly unlikely that anyone could get their head cut off in this or any other elevator door. I decided it would limit my employment potential to mention this.

We took the not-so-haunted elevator to the second floor, which had a wide hallway with six rooms on each side. Henry took me into one of the unoccupied rooms. It was on the small side, only large enough to fit a queen bed and a side table on one wall, with a petite armoire crammed on the opposite wall, and a bathroom carved out of a corner. From all I could tell, there were no ghosts present.

Henry took me to the third floor, which was much like the second. All the while, Henry peppered me with questions about my background. I did a respectable job sharing my rehearsed stories about who I was and where I was from. Finally, he took me to the roof.

The elevator opened onto a ten-by-twenty-foot observation platform, no more than an oversize balcony, with ornate wrought iron railings encircling it. Henry had placed four teak benches at the edge of the observation platform, so his guests could sit and admire the spectacular view down to the valley. "Welcome to the widow's walk. Guests love to come up here in the evening to watch the sun set. It's absolutely stunning," Henry said, taking in the view.

"It's amazing now, I can imagine it's even better at sunset." I took in the impressive view. From this vantage point, I could see some of the town off to one side and Castlerock Road and Grimly Flats off to the other. It was, in a word, spectacular.

After an uneventful tour, we were back at the front desk.

"It's a lot scarier at night," he said, by way of apology.

I bet it was, especially after a few nightcaps.

"Thanks very much for your time and the tour. So, about the job ..."

"Yes, of course. We'd love to have you. Kathy's moving to Wendlewood. She's been great. It's hard replacing such a stellar employee." I looked over at Kathy, who was within earshot. She was smiling and pretending she wasn't listening to Henry. She was probably grinning because she wouldn't have to wear the awful polyester jacket and floppy bow tie once she left.

Henry and I discussed the details of my employment and how given Kathy's sudden departure, I'd need to start fairly soon. I also considered—but not out loud— my need to prove to Victor I was serious about getting and keeping a job. We decided I should start on Thursday, which would be the first day of my weekly schedule going forward. I hoped this gig wouldn't end as abruptly as the last. After all, there were only so many guys I could injure in their most delicate spot before the rumor mill started working overtime.

After I left the hotel, I stopped at the café for a little lunch. I told myself it wasn't because I hoped to run into Luke, but I was pleasantly surprised to see him when I walked in the door.

For once, the diner wasn't jammed with people. I looked around for Bette, but she was nowhere to be found. In fact, there wasn't a single customer in the restaurant. I poked my head around the corner into the kitchen.

"Where is everyone?" I asked Luke.

"They're up at the church. Reverend Dickenson is having a memorial service for Mrs. Stramtussle and Mrs. Heard. Were you invited?"

"Nope. Were you?"

"It was more important that Bette went, so I decided to keep the café open in case someone wandered in, rather than closing it down for the day."

"I'm glad you did because I'm starving."

"I bet I can help with that." When Luke looked my way, those alluring blue eyes rattled me. He could help me with so many things—but none of them were appropriate in a café at noon.

"What are you making?" I asked, looking over his shoulder.

"Do you like pastrami?"

"Do I ever! I used to go to this deli—" I stopped myself. I couldn't tell him about my favorite delicatessen on the Lower East Side. "Well, anyway, it was the best."

I reached over to steal a little sliver of meat, but he playfully slapped my hand away. Even that brief touch sent a zap of electricity through me.

"You've got to be patient," Luke joked as he wagged his index finger in front of me with a grin. I was tempted to bite it, but resisted. "When Bette was ordering, I had her pick up some rye bread." He pulled a loaf from the shelf next to him.

"We need spicy brown mustard! Do you have any?" I asked.

"You'll have to get into my special stash. Bette doesn't like to order that—she thinks yellow mustard is absolutely fine for her customers."

"Sacrilege!" I shouted with fake outrage. "So, where can I find the good stuff?"

"Back in my locker, just past the sink."

I found Luke's locker and inside was a plastic bottle of Gulden's Spicy Brown Mustard—the good stuff–as expected. I didn't expect to find a loan application to purchase a property located at the corner of Grimly Flats and Castlerock Road. There it was, sitting right on top of the mustard. There was no way I could've found the mustard without seeing the documents.

Now I was baffled. Luke was trying to buy his farm. But from whom? The most logical person was Greta Stramtussle, who seemed to own all the property around here. I grabbed the mustard and returned to Luke, deciding to keep quiet about my discovery for now.

Luke piled the pastrami on the rye bread, then I squeezed mustard all over the meat. My mouth watered as Luke passed me the plates, which I took to a booth by the window.

"Beer?"

"Absolutely."

He brought two beers in frosty mugs.

"Cheers," I said, raising my glass. "Kudos to the chef!"

Luke raised his glass to meet mine before we dove into our sandwiches. This was one of the best moments I'd had since I'd been here. The cold beer, the delicious sandwich, and of course, the company wasn't bad either.

"Luke, this is the best sandwich I've had in my life."

"I seriously doubt that. But thank you." Luke took a hearty bite. "Yeah, that's pretty damn delicious if I do say so myself."

We demolished our sandwiches, finished our beers, and talked a little throughout. He was surprisingly easy to be with.

"Another beer?" Luke asked.

"Are you trying to get me drunk?" That was the wrong thing to say.

"No, I was just trying to be nice."

"Yes, I know. I'm sorry, I shouldn't have said that." Me and my big fat mouth getting me into trouble again. I checked the time. It was just a few minutes before school got out. "Actually, while I really would love to stay and have another beer with you, I need to pick up Allie from school. But thanks for lunch. What do I owe you?"

"Owe me? This one's on me."

"Thanks," I said as I went to the door, my head in the clouds. There was just one problem—what was Luke doing with a loan application in his locker, and what did it mean for the murder investigation?

FIFTEEN

I'd promised Allie this would be the last time I'd pick her up since we were both going to Flora Lane's after school. In the future, I'd trust she could make her way there without me, although the thought of it made my stomach lurch. As I arrived at the school, I kept well back from the chain-link fence, instead lurking behind a telephone pole. When I spotted Allie playing handball, I was relieved to see her having fun with other kids. Maybe she was starting to fit in.

I turned around and ran into Sam Ferrell. I shuffled backward to avoid being so close to him. I had no idea how he'd react to me after what happened on my first—and last—day of employment at the feed store.

"And what brings you down here, Ruby?" Sam asked, his gaze drifting down the length of my body in a way that made me feel like a piece of meat at the butcher's counter.

"I was here to pick up my daughter, not that it's any of your business."

"I cut your check for that day you worked for me. Jus' trying to be fair to you. So, why don't you stop by the feed store to pick it up?"

There was no way on God's green earth I was going to step foot in the feed store, even to pick up my measly paycheck.

"I appreciate you trying to be fair. I heard you're on the school board, so if we are going to talk about being fair, then I'd like to see if I can bring the case of my daughter's grade placement to the school board."

"You want some sort of a hearing? We don't do that. You see, we jus' do things like deciding when the ice cream social is."

"Well, Mrs. Heard said—"

"May she rest in peace," he interrupted, trying, for my benefit, to act like a God-fearing and completely blameless sexual harasser.

"I'm so sorry about her passing, but yes, I would like to talk with the school board. You see, my daughter—"

"I'm sure you can tell me all about it when you come to the meeting. Next Monday night. Seven o'clock. You'll be first on the agenda," he said as he ambled away.

"I'd like to get my paycheck when I see you at the meeting, so I don't have to disturb you at work," I shouted after him.

The school bell rang. Allie saw me, grabbed the ball, and then handed it to a tall girl with shaggy blond hair standing next to her.

"Bye, Alley Cat!" the girl called as Allie rushed toward me, a smile on her face.

Allie turned and hollered back, "Bye, Loud Mouth Lucy." Wow. I was glad Allie had such a mild nickname. I'd have been mortified if she'd come home and told me that everyone was calling her "Annoying Allie." I'd take Alley Cat any day of the week. It was cute.

"Lucy and I want to hang out tomorrow. Is that okay?" Allie asked.

"Sure, honey, but I'll need to ask her mom."

"We already did. Lucy's mom works in the office." Of course. Allie had become friends with a Stramtussle.

I popped into the office.

Meg Stramtussle was just hanging up the phone.

"Hi. My daughter, Allie, said she wanted to set up a playdate with your daughter."

"Oh sure, the girls already checked with me. That would be nice."

Meg and I exchanged contact information and made plans to get the girls together after school.

On our way to Flora's shop, I pointed out various landmarks to Allie, like the animal shelter and the café. She said nothing as we strolled. I was sure she was internally rolling her eyes, knowing, of course, the way around this postage-stamp town.

We made the turn down the little alley next to the hardware store and heard a loud *bang* from the yard behind Flora's shop. We dashed through the store and into the yard to find Flora standing in the middle of a junk pile, a welder's helmet tipped back on her head, and a wisp of gray smoke encircling her.

"Yee-ha! Got that old TIG welder working again."

"You're okay?" I asked.

"Of course I am! I'm a professional," Flora said with a firm nod, which knocked the welding helmet down over her face. "Who turned out the lights?"

I rushed to her and helped her take off the mask.

"You're sure you're okay?"

"Yes, yes. I'm fine. I was just joshing about turning out the lights, you know. I've been doing this work since before you were born." Flora spotted Allie, who had stepped back and was now pressed against the shop's exterior wall. "And this must be your daughter."

Flora shoved the welding helmet into my hands and approached Allie. She didn't say a word, just stood still looking up at Flora. My kid had met many crazy artists over the years, so meeting someone new and eccentric never seemed to faze her.

"Well now, how do you do, miss—what should I call you?"

"Um, my name is Allie," she said in a barely audible voice.

"What? You've gotta try harder than that, my dear. These old ears aren't so good, especially now that they're ringing from that bang." She stuck her index finger in her ear and gave it a wiggle.

Allie's eyes flitted to me, then back to Flora.

"My name is Allie," she said in a much louder, confident voice.

"Ah, well, Allie. That's a fine name. Here, let's head inside. Maybe I can find a cookie for you." Allie followed Flora into the cottage behind the shop. I brought up the rear, leaving the welding helmet on a cluttered workbench outside. I found them in Flora's kitchen, or maybe it was a laboratory. It was frankly hard to tell. Since I was more than a little concerned about anything that Flora cooked in that kitchen, I was glad to see her pull out an unopened package of Oreos. She doled out a couple to each of us. Until recently, I would have said no to an Oreo, but what the heck—I needed to get used to the fact that I'd not be getting organic shortbread cookies from the upscale bakery a block from my studio like we used to.

"I expect you have homework. So, if you want to set yourself up right over here." Flora guided Allie to a roll top desk and, using her forearm, pushed aside what must've been a month's worth of mail, many with past-due stamps on their envelopes. She pulled out a chair, wiped off a few stray flecks of something that looked like ashes, and offered the chair to my daughter. Allie's eyes once again darted to me. I thought she needed reassurance that everything was fine. I was beginning to worry about that myself. I gave her a little nod of assurance.

Allie slid into the proffered chair and got to work.

"And now for you, Ruby. Are you staying or going?"

"I'm going to take off, but I'll be back in a couple of hours. Before I forget, Allie's got a playdate tomorrow, so we'll start officially on Thursday." I called to Flora, but there was no answer. She was too busy giving Allie the grand tour of all the treasures held within the shop's four walls. My daughter gazed wide-eyed at the stuffed jackalope, vintage farming equipment, antique glass vases, and oodles of other things too strange to identify.

I called Darla on my way out and told her I had some new information about Luke. She was at the thrift shop, so I headed over. When I arrived, she was sorting through some housewares someone had dropped off.

"Oh—I like those orange throw pillows," I said as she tossed them in an oversize basket. I retrieved them from the bin, set them next to a chair, and took a seat. They were going to be perfect for the living room sofa. "What do they cost?"

"I don't know. I usually just make up the prices. How about five dollars for both of them?"

"That works for me," I said, pulling a five out of my wallet and putting it on the counter next to me. "After all, I'm a working woman now."

"Hilltop Hotel?"

"How'd you know?" I asked.

"Word gets around," Darla said, cracking a smile. "So, you said you had some news for me."

"It's about Luke."

"Seems like you two are getting along nicely." Darla gave me a knowing wink.

"What? How do you know that?"

"Gossip central, haven't you figured that out yet?"

"Seriously?"

"No, I saw you two eating sandwiches at the café on my way here."

I picked up one of my new pillows and threw it at her. She tossed it back.

"So, what have you learned?"

"I accidentally found a loan application for the purchase of the farm where Luke lives."

"And how did you *accidentally* find it?"

"I was looking for mustard."

"Mm-hmm," Darla said, looking at me with a single eyebrow raised.

"True, I swear. Girl Scouts honor," I said holding up the traditional three-finger salute.

"You weren't a Girl Scout. No way."

"Actually, I was. And, I really wish I understood what that loan application was about," I said, releasing my salute.

"Did you happen to see which bank was issuing the loan?"

"No, but I don't think the loan is complete. There were no signatures or official stamps," I said.

"Interesting. I have no idea how that loan would fit into the deaths of Mrs. Stramtussle or Mrs. Heard."

"Who owns the property where Luke's farm is? Mrs. Stramtussle owned the houses on Castlerock and pretty much everywhere else in town. So maybe he was trying to buy the property from her."

"Maybe she wouldn't sell the property to him, and he got angry and killed her," Darla said.

"There's more ... Luke doesn't have an alibi for the night of the hayride."

"That, combined with the pitchfork, plus somehow the loan application ..." Darla bit her lip, thinking about how to fit the pieces of the puzzle together. "You're just going to have to find out more."

"Me?"

"Yeah, you're the one who's going to see Luke again."

"I am?"

"If you want to help me with this case, I'd say so. And with the way you were smiling at him at the café, I'm sure it won't be a chore for you."

I took a deep breath.

"I'll just have to find a reason to go to the farm, and then I can do some snooping around while I'm there."

"Hmm. Maybe Luke will invite you." Darla gave me a knowing nod.

"I'll report back when I have more intel," I said, giving her another three-finger salute as I stood by the door.

Darla cracked a smile and threw my two new pillows at me, which I grabbed midair as I ducked out the door.

SIXTEEN

On Wednesday, I had the whole day to myself. Allie left in the morning on her solo journey to school and that afternoon she had a playdate with Lucy Stramtussle-Sweet. The poor girl had been saddled with an unfortunate last name, which Meg and Dr. Dan could have easily avoided by choosing one or the other of their monikers. Since Meg's job in the administration office ended thirty minutes after school let out, the girls would be walking home with her.

I took my second cup of coffee to the porch behind the house, breathed in the warm sage-scented air, and exhaled. It was such a lovely moment to relax—one of the few I'd had in recent weeks—and I watched in silence as two rust-colored bunnies with white tails ran across the ground, stopping to nibble the leaves of some scrubby plants before running for cover as a hawk soared overhead.

I fantasized about my garden oasis and hoped I'd not have to bunny-proof my future vegetable patch with wire mesh and fencing. I knew I'd never resort to Elmer Fudd's method of *hunting wabbits* with a shotgun to control critters. I'd had enough of guns for the rest of my life after that disastrous night in Las Vegas.

After Ricky fired the gun, my sister and I ran for the elevator, chucking our high heels as we sprinted down the hall. Ricky ran towards us, the gun still in his hand. We pounded on the elevator call button in a panic. As he approached, we realized that the elevator was not coming fast enough, so we dashed for the stairs, stumbling over each other as we went down.

I shook off the terrible memories and focused on the present —my garden and my house. I had a full, glorious day all to myself, and I wasn't going to let any awful memories bring me down.

I checked my compost pile, pulling back the tarp Luke and I had laid on top of it. A wisp of steam escaped, and I felt the warmth from the decomposition of the veggie scraps. That was good sign.

Suddenly, a snake emerged from under the tarp and slithered past my feet. Fortunately, I had my trusty Keds on, and leaped backward so he couldn't sink his fangs into me. Holy crap! That was a close one. I was all alone, with no neighbors, and who knew how long it would take for an ambulance to arrive in case I'd been bitten. I quickly snapped a picture of the departing reptile with my phone. Whew! I had really dodged a bullet—or snake. I wasn't sure I'd ever get used to living here. And where was Boomer? Not around to protect me, that was certain. Luke's cat Peaches wasn't the only slacker pet in Paradise.

My childhood had seemed so much easier. I hadn't been afraid of snakes, or any other animal for that matter. It had been all those years in New York that had made me cautious about of everything—people most of all.

I hadn't let too many people into my life. I had few buddies, mostly studio-mates who were friends of convenience. I'd been close to Claudia when we were children since we were just two years apart. We were inseparable. Since I was the older sibling, I was always held to a higher standard. Claudia, on the other hand, could get away with almost anything. She was the baby, and the apple of my father's eye. After we'd both left the farm, we stayed in touch and got together when we could.

I pulled out a box of vintage glass bottles from the shed, working slowly to ensure no surprise critters jumped out at me. Relieved I hadn't run across any other uninvited—or scary—guests, I took the bottles upstairs to the front porch where there was a water spigot and a bucket. I grabbed a sponge from the kitchen and got to work on the bottles. They were a myriad of shapes, in clear and cobalt glass—except some had turned a pale lavender, a sure sign that they were antique. As I washed each bottle, I placed them on the bench next to me to dry. It was quite a collection, though I wasn't sure what I would do with them. Perhaps I'd simply put them on the windowsill and admire the beauty of their shapes and colors.

Finished with my task, and slightly damp from all the scrubbing, I stood to admire my work. I stretched my back, which was aching from crouching over a bucket. As I did, a dusty red pickup truck pulled up in front of my house.

"Hello, ma'am," Luke said, squinting up at me now that the sun had crested the roof of the house.

"You know I prefer Ruby, right?" I said, squinting back at him in exasperation.

"I do, but I like the way you get all riled up when I call you ma'am." He got out of the truck's cab and came toward me. "What have you got there?" Luke asked, pointing to my row of bottles.

"I found them in the shed. I think they're pretty, but I'm not sure what I'm going to do with them."

"They'd be good for some propagation. Fill them up with water, add cuttings, and you'll have new plants in no time," Luke said. "Come on, I'll take you down to my farm and show you how."

"That would be amazing." This was an offer I simply couldn't refuse. It was a chance to start my succulent garden. I hoped it would also give me a chance to ask him some questions about the loan document I'd seen in his locker at the café. There were other reasons that were less than squeaky-clean, but I set those aside in the name of sleuthing and gardening.

I got my purse and locked the front door, glad I wasn't too grubby to go with Luke, and slid into the passenger seat of his truck.

"I can get some succulent cuttings for you while we're at my farm," Luke said, pulling away from the curb.

"I was going to ask, but now that you've offered ..."

"You should never be shy about asking for something you want," Luke said.

I was glad he was staring straight ahead while driving because if he'd been looking at me, I think I might have melted into the seat. Seriously, I was going to remember—and take—his advice the next time I had the chance.

Luke pulled his truck onto a gravel parking area near Grimly Flats Road. On the far side of the property was an old adobe house, larger than I'd realized when I'd seen it from the street the night of the hayride.

"Welcome to my little farm," Luke said, beaming. He looked around, proud of what he'd created on this land. "Let me give you a tour."

Luke took me by the hand—I tried not to hyperventilate—and showed me his garden and all the amazing things he was growing.

"Here we've got the sempervivum—the common name is houseleek. They like a little sun and to be squished in close together," Luke said as we admired a flat black tray of tiny gray-green rosettes, one of many on a table. "I'll be taking all of those to the sell at the swap meet in Phoenix on Sunday."

"Wow, that's a long trip."

"But it's worth it. I sell out every time. I don't get back until really late on Sunday nights, so I'm exhausted during the breakfast shift at Bette's Place on Monday mornings."

Next, we walked through his vegetable garden with rows and rows of new sprouts.

"Do you have any fruit trees?" I asked.

"No. I don't want to plant any trees unless I know I'm going to stay."

"Why wouldn't you stay?"

"Because I don't own this land. I've been trying to buy it, but haven't had any luck."

"I didn't mean to be nosy, but I saw a loan application when I got the mustard out of your locker. Does that have something to do with it?"

"It's no secret I've been trying to buy this plot of land. I made an offer and got approved for a loan, but Greta Stramtussle told me she had another buyer. I never found out if that was true or if she was just trying to get me to increase my offer before she died."

"I'm sorry," I said. "Maybe one of Greta's kids will want to sell you the land."

"We'll see—but listen, you didn't come over to hear my tale of woe. You want to see something really great?"

"Absolutely!"

"This is where I'm doing some propagation," Luke said, guiding me to a table full of pots that sat under a canopy of shade cloth.

"That just looks like a bunch of leaves sitting in soil," I said, wondering what the heck he thought he could accomplish that way. I certainly had seen plenty of leaves on the ground, and not a single one had ever grown into a tree.

"You have to look closely," Luke said, pulling me in tight so we could look at the leaves. "See the sprouts?"

Sure enough, tiny new plants were growing from the ends of the leaves. I gasped in delight and turned toward Luke, who took my moment of astonishment to surprise me with a kiss. Possibly the best kiss ever. My heart galloped, and I worried briefly I may have a heart attack, but at least I'd die happy.

I staggered backward, out of his embrace.

"I'm sorry, ma'am, maybe I wasn't supposed to do that," he said as he broke into a slow, sexy smile.

"Ruby," I whispered in his ear. "And yes, you can do that anytime."

"Well now," Luke said, shaking off some of our intensity. "No visit is complete to my farm without meeting Miss Peaches."

Luke clapped three times, and a fat calico cat came running.

"Well hello, Peaches," I exclaimed, as I reached down to pet her. She rubbed back and forth across my ankles, purring up a storm.

"I think she likes you," Luke said.

"The feeling is mutual." What I really wanted to say was, Luke, will you be my boyfriend? But it seemed a bit soon to ask that, and I'd also told myself that a boyfriend was out of the question.

"Now, let's get you set up to do some propagation of your own. I'm going to send you home with some leaves and cuttings and you can start your own little succulent farm. For the cuttings, fill those pretty bottles of yours with water and put a cutting in each one. For the leaves, just place them flat on the soil in a pot, and mist them whenever the soil dries out. Then put them where they'll get a little sunshine, like your back porch. Not too much sun, or they'll fry." Luke filled a paper bag with cuttings and leaves and handed it to me as I left.

"Are you sure you don't want me to drive you back to your house?"

"Of course not. I could use the walk."

"Watch out for snakes," Luke shouted as I ambled to the road. I stopped in my tracks and marched back to him, pulling out my phone as I did. I pulled up the picture of the snake that attacked me—well, just sort of slithered by me.

"Do you know what kind of snake this is? It was under the tarp near the compost pile. What do you think? A rattlesnake? Do I need to get a snake trapper, or—"

"That's just a gopher snake. He's one of the good guys."

Luke did not laugh. I was thankful for that. I wanted to tell him *he* was one of the good guys, but held back. I didn't want to ruin a perfect day by saying something stupid.

"Well, thank you! I wouldn't want to die of a snakebite," I said as I turned back toward home.

"And neither would I."

Holy smokes. I had never enjoyed a visit to a farm so much in my life.

SEVENTEEN

I called Darla as I walked in the front door of my house. Boomer leaped at my feet like he'd been found after weeks alone on a deserted island.

"I've got some news for you," I told her when she picked up. "Luke was trying to buy his farmland from Mrs. Stramtussle, but she told him she'd gotten another offer and told him no."

"I guess that's good news and bad news," Darla said. "It makes sense that the land was owned by Mrs. Stramtussle, but we don't know who the other potential buyer of the property is."

"If there even is one. It's possible Mrs. Stramtussle didn't have another buyer but was trying to get more money out of Luke or something," I said.

"Well, she's not around to ask," Darla said, a note of frustration in her voice.

"I know, but little by little we'll figure it out."

"I do have a question for you though."

"Yes?"

"How'd everything go with Luke?"

"What kind of nosy question is that? I'm not one to kiss and tell."

"What!?"

"Meet me at Bette's Place tomorrow for lunch? I can fill you in then."

I spent the rest of my day setting up my succulent babies on the back porch.

Around seven, I left for Meg's house with Boomer in tow. Actually, it was more like I was in tow because Boomer dragged me along. Clearly, I needed to get him out for walks more often. Boomer zigged and zagged across the narrow streets as we went, and at one point, barked at a small gray feral cat with a tipped ear. There were still a few wild cats in town, even with all of Mrs. Stramtussle's trapping and Dr. Sweet's neutering and spaying.

Meg and Lucy lived at the tippy-top of the hill in Paradise. It was a long, but invigorating walk for me. I arrived out of breath and in need of something to drink.

"Come in!" Meg said. A chubby toddler peeked out from behind her legs. I leaned down and gave the little boy a smile and a wave. By the sounds coming from the family room, Lucy and Allie were playing some sort of interactive video game. I settled in at the kitchen table with Meg and the baby.

"So, what brought you to Paradise?" Meg asked, pouring me a glass of lemonade and popping her baby into his high chair almost simultaneously. Her ability to multitask was impressive.

There it was—the dreaded question.

"You know, we'd heard it was a nice place. We just wanted something different."

"Sure. I get it. Did you just get divorced?"

"Um, no ... my ex hasn't been in the picture for quite some time." This seemed like a giant leap for her to make. There could be hundreds of reasons why I'd move to a new town, though divorce did seem like a valid reason.

"It's just that I'm divorced, so I totally get it. You end up a single mom, you need to make a change. Unfortunately for me, I wasn't able to up and move away. At least my ex-husband is here in town, so he can do some babysitting now and then. Have you met him—Dr. Dan Sweet? His office is across from the hardware store."

"Yes, I have. He told me you two were divorced. Little by little I'm figuring out how everyone is connected in this town."

"It's easy, everyone is connected. *Everyone*," Meg said. "And all the ladies just love Dr. Dan. Unfortunately, he decided to love one back."

"Got it. So, you kept your maiden name?"

"Yep. I mean, who would want to be Meg Sweet? I would sound like some sort of holiday eggnog drink." We both laughed at that. But if it had been me, I'd have gotten rid of *Stramtussle* in a heartbeat. Meg Sweet, that was short and sweet. After all, when I'd had the opportunity to change my name, I went from Patricia Martinez to Ruby Shaw. My new name was uncomplicated—like I wanted my life to be—though I felt sad I'd left my Mexican roots behind when I chose my new name.

"He told me about the work he did with your mother and the feral cats."

The baby banged his hands on the high chair tray, and Meg gave him another bit of cookie to chew on.

"Gus is a handful, but that's a good thing. A baby and a divorce in just a matter of months. On top of that, my mother passing in such a horrible way just days ago. It's been a helluva year."

"My sympathies for the loss of your mother. This *has* been a terrible time for you." I didn't know Meg well—not at all, actually—so I wasn't sure if I should hug her or something else. I opted for a pat on the hand.

"Yeah, well, it's sort of a mixed blessing, to be honest."

"What?"

"She loved her feral cats more than her own family. Here I was, struggling to make ends meet, marriage on the rocks, and did she help me? The answer is no. No, she didn't." Meg's cheery exterior melted away as she considered the loss of her mother. "But we don't have to talk about all that horrible stuff." She pasted on a smile and took a dainty sip of her lemonade.

"I'm sorry for your loss," I repeated, not sure what else I could say. I wanted to quiz Meg about where she'd been the night her mother died. Could Meg be a cold-blooded killer? She undeniably had a reason. It seemed she could use the money, especially being a newly single mother with two kids. Speeding her mother's demise along might have been a way for her to cash in on the Stramtussle estate and give her the financial stability she clearly needed.

"I'm sorry about Mrs. Heard too. To lose two important women in your life—that's got to be hard."

"You tell me—how were your interactions with Mrs. Heard?" Meg asked, a sharpness in her voice I hadn't expected.

"The last time I talked with her we had an argument about Allie's placement test."

"I know! That was par for the course for her. That was a weekly occurrence. She wasn't the beloved principal she appeared to be."

This was news to me.

"I'm just curious. You know the day we came into the office to sign Allie up for school, Mrs. Heard couldn't find her red glasses. Do you remember that?"

"Do I ever! She hounded me about those damn glasses for days. She accused me of stealing them—imagine that. I'd just lost my mother, and had come to work to distract myself from the depression I was suffering. There was Mrs. Heard, ransacking my desk looking for her glasses. It was insane! She never did find them."

"Darla Cotton said Mrs. Heard never came back after setting

up the pumpkins at the hayride. Did you see her at the end of the day?" I asked.

"No, but I left early and took the kids to their dad's, so if she came back, I wasn't at the office."

Just then, the baby started crying, and Boomer leaped up and barked, sending the boy into an even higher volume of sobbing.

"Is that Ricky, my mom's dog?" She gave her son another piece of cookie, and he calmed down a little, but I could tell he wasn't going to be happy in his high chair for much longer.

"As a matter of fact, it is."

"We've been looking for him," Meg reached down to pet the dog, who returned her affection with several licks. My stomach lurched. Could Meg want the dog? Allie would be devastated to lose Boomer now.

"Darla Cotton told us he needed a home, so we adopted him."

"Maybe she should have asked me first," Meg said, grabbing his collar and protectively pulling the dog toward her. He looked up at her and wagged his tail.

"Allie's become really attached to Boomer." I clenched my jaw at the thought of losing the dog.

"Boomer? This is Ricky—didn't Darla tell you that?"

"She did, but we didn't really like that name." I certainly couldn't tell that I'd watched someone named Ricky kill a man in cold blood just a few weeks before.

"You can have him, I've already got my hands full. But just so you know, that dog meant the world to my mom. So, if I ever hear you've not been treating him well, then I *will* take him away from you." Her voice was taut with certainty. I knew she'd be someone I could never cross—a real mama bear. I could relate; I was one as well.

"So, are you working? Pretty tough getting a job around here," Meg said, thankfully changing the subject.

"I'm going to be working at the Hilltop Hotel."

"And who's looking after Allie?"

"I've got her set up with Flora Lane. She seems nice, though a little eccentric," I said, thinking that I'd already made a commitment to her, but wondering if that had been the right decision.

"You want to stay away from her. She's a few crayons short of a box." Just then, the baby reached for Meg, his cookie crumbled in bits on the high chair tray and all over his hands and face. "Sorry, I need to get Gus cleaned up! I'll send Allie out," Meg said, hoisting the baby from his chair and rushing off.

"Are you ready to go?" I asked Allie, as I opened the door to let ourselves out. Allie beamed and nodded. Whew! It seemed like the playdate had gone well.

I was glad Boomer was coming home with us. I opted not to tell Allie about Meg's attachment to the dog, since I didn't want to worry her unnecessarily about him being taken from us.

I wondered what Meg meant about Flora. I was usually a good judge of character—okay, maybe not a *great* judge—but I saw nothing seriously wrong with Flora. Perhaps Meg had some history with her, which wouldn't be surprising, given that everyone seemed to have a history with everyone else in Paradise.

On our way home, we heard the distant sound of coyotes howling. It was always a thrill for us, a reminder of where we were, in an utterly different place than the world we left behind. Most of the sounds we'd hear in New York around this time were the horns of taxi cabs during rush hour. The coyotes' yipping seemed much more soothing as we walked through town on this warm fall evening.

* * *

ONCE HOME, I gave Victor a call.

"Victor! Guess what?"

"You got a job," he replied.

"What a party pooper. You're supposed to let me tell you that, not guess. But you're right. I have a job." I told Victor about my job at the hotel and how I'd even located a babysitter for Allie. "And you know what else this means?"

"I already brought you a bag of dirt, two lamps and a computer," he said, an amused tone to his voice.

"Again, with the guessing. You're supposed to let me tell you!"

"I'm proud of you, Ruby. It looks like you and Allie are really settling in."

"Yes, but ..."

"But what?"

"Crazy things are happening here."

"What kind of crazy?"

"There was a hayride the other night—"

"Hayride? How quaint."

"Here's the not-so-quaint part. There was a spooky scene with a dummy who had been stabbed. Instead, it was real. The school principal had been attacked with a pitchfork, and was lying dead across a hay bale. I'm just wondering if the murder is connected to the one that happened the first night we arrived."

"You can stop wondering," Victor said.

"Why? Because you know that they *are*?"

"Of course not. That's not my department. My department is keeping innocent folks safe. Just as long as they stay innocent, got it?"

"Got it. But—"

"No *buts*. I want you to go about your business. Work on your garden."

"I've got my very own cactus—it's not in a pot yet, but it's a start. And I have some cuttings that I got from Luke."

"Luke?"

"He's the cook at the local café, and also a farmer."

"You're making friends right and left, aren't you?" He didn't know just how close a friend Luke was rapidly becoming. I returned to the subject of cacti. "Succulents come in all of these fun shapes and colors—and it's really difficult to kill them. And I've got myself a compost pile, but that's not enough. Though, I could use some wood to make a nice compost bin and lid to hold it and a big roll of shade cloth…."

"Compost bin? Shade cloth? You really are going to become a farmer, like your new friend Luke?"

"Well, maybe not a farmer, but some sort of gardener. You know … a horticulturist!"

"Horticulturist?" Victor snorted and laughed. "I've never known anyone who had that as a job!"

"You've probably never met an astronaut, and I can assure you that's a real job. Besides, I'm also working at the hotel, so I have my bases covered," I said, proud that after my false start at the feed store, I was finally getting settled into a job. "So, any chance I can get some of those garden supplies?"

"You show me you can keep a job, I'll see what I can do about your requests," Victor said. There was lightness in his voice, like he was pleased we were getting acclimated. "And how is Allie doing? Did you get things sorted out at school?"

"I'm still working on that. She's made a new friend, so that's helped a lot. Another Stramtussle."

"Stramtussle? As in the woman who died next door?"

"Her granddaughter, Lucy. This town is lousy with Stram-tussles."

"Just try and stay away from them. They're going to make your life complicated," Victor said. It was good advice that I doubted I could follow.

EIGHTEEN

Thursday was my first day at the Hilltop Hotel. I stopped at Bette's Place for lunch before my shift started. I took a seat in a booth to wait for Darla. Within minutes, Bette was in front of me with a mug and a pot of steaming coffee, but she'd lost her usual cheery disposition. While she moved quickly, her smile was missing.

"What's wrong?" I asked.

"I can't talk about it here, sugar," she replied, in a shaky voice. I noticed there was no engagement ring on her hand. Uh-oh. Had her engagement with Derek Stramtussle already ended? If so, that would possibly be one of the shortest engagements in history.

That Derek Stramtussle was a piece of work. I liked Bette, but I had to wonder why she'd want him. He seemed sort of creepy to me, just a little too slick to be trusted. She had to know about him. Everyone knew everything about everybody. And that worried me—if someone found out who I really was, everyone would know within a matter of days, make that hours. If that happened, I had no doubt Victor would move us to a new town. I didn't want that. This quirky town had grown on me, and Allie was happier than I'd seen her in weeks.

"I'm worried about you. Will you come over to my house after I get off work? I want to hear about what happened," I said.

"Maybe I'll find my ring by then."

"I hope so, but if not, please visit me—maybe I can help. I'm starting my job at the Hilltop Hotel today, but I'll be home and waiting for you after seven."

It looked like getting tangled in the web of gossip that the town ran on was inevitable. But gossip aside, I was concerned about Bette. She was usually such a ray of sunshine. Seeing her this upset really worried me. We made a plan for her to visit me after my shift.

Darla arrived a few minutes later and we both ordered Reuben sandwiches for lunch, not really a healthful choice, but it reminded me of the deli I used to go to in my old neighborhood. I missed New York, but somehow, it had become more of an abstraction, not so much a real place to me as it once had been.

"I got some results back from the lab on the piece of plastic you found. They won't have time for a couple of weeks to do DNA testing, but it's definitely the temple from a pair of eyeglasses." Darla said. "But I'm still not sure they belong to Mrs. Heard. Last Friday when I went to see her—the day of the hayride—she wasn't in the office and neither was Meg, so I have no confirmation that those glasses belonged to Mrs. Heard."

"But I do! I asked Meg about them when I picked up Allie from a playdate."

"And?"

"Mrs. Heard most definitely had lost her red glasses. Apparently, she gave Meg quite a bad time about it—accused her of stealing them," I said. "So that piece *must* be from Mrs. Heard's glasses."

"Looks that way. Though it doesn't really help us much. Now that she's dead, she's no longer a suspect."

"She could have killed Mrs. Stramtussle, and then someone turned around and killed her," I said.

"True, but I somehow think it was the same person. I mean, how many killers could we have in this town?"

That was an excellent question.

After lunch, I waved at Luke in the kitchen as Darla and I left.

"So, are you going to tell me what happened with you and Luke?" Darla asked.

"Oh! Look at the time. I've got to run, or I'll be late for my first day on the job."

"I can't believe you're not going to tell me," Darla said with a heavy sigh.

"Maybe someday!"

* * *

I ARRIVED at the Hilltop Hotel at one o'clock. Henry met me at the front desk and gave me the standard-issue black polyester blazer along with a silky bow to wear around the collar of my blouse. They were horrifying. I was a good sport and put them on, looking sufficiently funereal to work at a haunted hotel.

I spent the afternoon learning how to check people into their rooms on the computer. That was easy. It was a challenge when I realized that hauling patrons' luggage to their rooms was also part of my job description. Fortunately, there were only a few customers that day, but I could imagine how difficult it might be if the hotel had no vacancies. I hoped when that happened Henry might see his way clear to hiring a bellman.

On a break, I called Flora to make sure Allie had made it to her shop safe and sound. Flora said, yes, of course Allie was with her and had been a great help in locating a rattlesnake, then abruptly hung up the phone. A rattlesnake. I really didn't want to know what that was about. Perhaps Meg Stramtussle was right—Flora was insane. I could only hope she was crazy in a good way.

About an hour before my shift was to end, Henry showed up at the front desk to see how things were going.

"Fine, no problems. I haven't had any issues with the computer or helping customers. Everything's great," I said. Just then, I spotted one of the guests, Mrs. Hess, chugging toward me down the hall. She arrived at the front desk with a beet-red face and a grimace. This would be my first customer service challenge, and I had to do it while my new boss watched.

"We haven't seen a single ghost. We were promised paranormal phenomena," Mrs. Hess smacked her palms on the reception counter. "Why else would we stay in a haunted hotel?" she asked indignantly. Before I could say a word, Henry took over. Rats! I'd already blown it.

"I'm sorry about that. Sometimes the spirits take a little while to settle down before they appear," Henry said.

What a load of crap.

"Why don't you sit right here in this comfy chair." Henry guided the woman to an overstuffed chair with a good view down the short hall to the elevators. "Ruby, why don't you get Mrs. Hess a glass of port? Wouldn't you like that?" he asked the woman.

Mrs. Hess nodded appreciatively from her seat while Henry returned to his place behind the counter. As I passed Henry with the glass of port, he slipped his hand under the countertop and discretely pressed a button. I presented Mrs. Hess with her glass of port, and as I turned, I saw the elevator doors open, close, and then the elevator began to ascend. We watched as the arrow ticked up past each floor number and then down again on the dial above the door. The elevator doors opened again, with no one on board.

Mrs. Hess gasped and tossed back her port.

"Was that the ghost you told me about, who rides the elevator each night around this time?" Mrs. Hess asked Henry.

Henry gave her a knowing nod. "Yes, it might be."

Satisfied, Mrs. Hess returned to her room a few minutes later, once it became clear that the invisible man wasn't going to repeat his trip.

I turned to Henry.

"Are you going to explain to me what the heck happened just now?"

"You've got to give them what they want. The guests are going to be disappointed if they don't see some sort of supernatural events when staying at a haunted hotel."

"And your little remote-controlled elevator stunt provides that."

"That, along with some other features."

"Do you mind telling me what other features?" I asked. I was getting more disgusted by the minute. Basically, this guy was a charlatan, a scam artist. He brought people to his hotel under false pretenses. His hotel wasn't what he claimed it to be, but then again, neither was I. However, I had reason to misrepresent myself—my life depended on it. But Henry? Did his life depend on it? I doubted it, but certainly, his livelihood could. If customers only came to see the hauntings, then he might not have a single paying guest without his special effects.

"Ah well, those are trade secrets," Henry said, wiping his sweaty brow with a handkerchief. "But as you continue to work here, I'll show you some of the other ways we enhance our guests' experience."

This seemed like a total charade to me. And the old version of me would have called him on it. The new me needed a job. I smiled and nodded. One thing was clear, I didn't feel nervous about being in a haunted hotel since it wasn't actually haunted.

NINETEEN

Having gotten off work a little early, I retrieved Allie from Flora's shop, and all the way home, Allie chattered about how much fun she'd had at the store. I was relieved to hear the snake was a taxidermy rattlesnake and not, in fact, a live one. I was also relieved that Flora seemed to be working out. It was a step in the right direction. I wasn't sure if the same could be said about me. While Allie had enjoyed being at Flora's, she hadn't gotten much homework done. After dinner, I sent her off to her bedroom to finish her assignments moments before a frazzled Bette showed up on my doorstep. She was in tears.

"Oh no! Bette! Please come in." I ushered her to the armchair, where she collapsed. "Let me get you something to drink." I dashed to the kitchen and was back a minute later with iced tea. "Here, drink this. You'll feel better if you do."

She drank and sat quietly. I wondered what awful things Derek Stramtussle had said to her.

"Now tell me, what did Derek do? Did he break up with you?" I asked once she'd calmed down enough to talk.

"What? No, of course not!"

"You're upset, and you don't have your ring on anymore, so I thought maybe you two had called off the wedding."

"No. It's not that at all. I lost my ring. Or maybe it's been stolen. I just don't know. But I've looked everywhere, and I simply can't find it."

"When was the last time you had it?"

"I took it off when I was working in the kitchen at the café. I thought I left it on the shelf above the sink, but maybe I put it in my pocket, I can't really remember. When I went back for it a little while later, it was gone."

This was a concern because the only other person who worked in the kitchen was Luke, and he was a friend. I hoped he wasn't a thief because my list of friends in this town was pretty short.

"Who do you think could have stolen it?"

"Luke's an obvious choice, but I don't think it's him. The thing is, customers have to pass by that shelf to get to the restroom, so any number of people could have seen it and swiped it on their way by."

Well, that undoubtedly would make it a challenge to figure out who the culprit was.

"Are you sure you wore it to work this morning?"

"Of course, but just to make sure, I went home and checked. It wasn't there." A sob welled up in Bette's voice.

"It couldn't have fallen in the sink?"

"Derek came over and pulled apart the whole U-bend on the sink. Nothing! He's as upset as I am."

"I'm sorry. I wish I could help, but I just don't know what to do. Maybe you could list it as missing online. Does Paradise have something like Craigslist?"

"No, we just have a bulletin board out in front of the restaurant. My feeling is it's gone for good. I'm wondering if it's a bad omen or something."

It was hard to pinpoint what I didn't like about Derek. I

guess I simply didn't trust him. He looked to be about ten years younger than Bette. Those two facts together made me wonder: What was his angle? What was he trying to achieve by marrying her? It seemed like he was always trying to sell something, a bit of a snake oil salesman. Bette had to know what he was like, after all, she was going to marry him. If I were Bette, I'd think twice about marrying this guy, but who was I to judge? I was hiding out from bad guys—some really, really bad guys—so I couldn't profess to having made the best decisions in my life. But actually, it was Claudia who hadn't made good choices. I just happened to have gotten caught in the cross fire.

"I've got to admit, I'm surprised you're marrying him. Sorry, I don't mean to be so bold, but he doesn't seem like your type."

"My type? How dare you! Are you sure you don't mean it's because I'm Black and he's white?"

"What? No, absolutely not! It's not like that at all. You're just an interesting couple. It's like opposites attract."

"You don't know how hard it's been," Bette broke down, sobbing. "Greta never liked me. Thought her son was too good for me. Now that's she's gone, Derek thought we finally could be together."

"I'm sorry, I didn't know. As long as you love him, it doesn't really matter what I think, or anybody else for that matter." I reached out to take Bette's hand, but she recoiled.

"It was a mistake to come here," Bette said, pulling out a hanky and wiping her eyes.

"No, I'm glad you did. It seems like you could use a friend. I'm sorry we had a moment there, and I really shouldn't have said that. I could use a friend too."

"I really should go," Bette said as she stood up and started pawing through her purse. "Dang it, where are my keys?"

"I think you had them in your hand when you came in." We looked around, under the coffee table and sofa, but there was no sign of her keys. Kneeling in front of the armchair, I shoved my hands between the cushion and the sides where Bette had been sitting, I ran my hands along the seams, until I came across something hard. Aha!

But it wasn't Bette's keys. I pulled out a ring—a wedding ring.

"Bette! I found your ring!" I shouted, jumping up and holding it out to her.

Excited, she grabbed it from me and took a good long look. Her mouth agape, she examined the ring in her hand.

"Only one problem. That's not my ring."

"What?"

"Not my ring. Unless I'm very much mistaken, that's Greta Stramtussle's ring. The one that went missing the night she died!" Bette looked at me, her eyes wide.

I was absolutely baffled. What was Greta Stramtussle's ring doing between my chair cushions? I certainly hadn't put it there.

"How can that be?" I grabbed the ring from Bette and looked at it closely. It was a wedding ring with a couple of carats' worth of diamonds in it. I'd never seen Mrs. Stramtussle's ring, so I couldn't be sure. But if Bette believed it, who was I to think otherwise? "I have no idea how it got here." I set it down on the coffee table, not wanting to touch it.

Bette squinted at me with suspicion. "I can't believe you'd do that!" I couldn't decipher what she was most upset about—that she might be in the same room as a murderer and ring thief or that I'd been stupid enough to pull it out and show it to her.

"I don't know how it got here. I swear. I seriously don't have any idea how or why it was in the armchair." I took a deep, calming breath.

"I think you need to turn yourself in to the sheriff," Bette said, clutching her handbag to her chest as if trying to protect herself from me.

"Why? I didn't do anything wrong. I have no idea how that ring got here."

"There's something fishy about you. You come here. No job. No husband," Bette said, pointing a shaky finger at me.

"Well, I, I …" I didn't know what to say. She was right. I could see how she, and likely everyone else in town, thought there was something weird about Allie and me. And frankly, they were right.

"I'll talk with law enforcement." I decided to leave things vague because I wasn't sure if I'd talk with Victor or Darla about this. I just hoped Victor wouldn't yank Allie and me out of town in response to my latest debacle.

Bette, now panicking, dumped the contents of her purse on the coffee table. There, among the used tissues, lipstick, and gum wrappers, were her keys. She gasped in relief when she found them and scooped everything back into her bag.

"I know this looks bad—" I started.

"You're darn right it does!" Bette said as she backed away from me. "You know what? I was trying real hard to be nice to you and your daughter. And now, I don't know what to think!"

"Why would I have pulled that ring out in front of you? I'd be a total idiot to do that!"

Bette paused as she reached the door. "That may be true, but there is something not right here. Not right at all." Bette turned and bolted out the door. I followed her out, watching as she sped away in her little two-door coupe, the wheels of the car squealing as they took the corner of each switchback.

I sat down on the front steps.

I pulled out my cell phone and called Victor.

"It's getting to be a regular thing, you calling me all the time," he said when he answered. "You know, you're going to have to figure out how to stand on your own two feet eventually."

"I know that. I'd love to! Stuff keeps happening beyond my control."

"What happened this time?" I could hear an impatient growl in his voice.

"Someone planted some evidence from the murder of my next-door neighbor in my house—in my armchair, to be exact."

"What did you find?"

"Mrs. Stramtussle's ring. It was missing when she turned up dead. I was searching in my upholstered chair for the local café owner's keys, and I found the ring. What's weird is that her engagement ring is also missing."

"Sounds like everyone in Paradise needs to be a little more careful with their fine jewelry," Victor said with a chuckle.

"Be serious. I don't want to get sucked into this mess."

"Sorry, sister, sounds like you already are. I think it may be time to pull you two out of there. Time to start again."

"No. Not yet. Allie's doing really well, and believe it or not, other than a few glitches—okay, more than a few—I like it here too. Is there anything you can do to smooth things out with the law enforcement here?"

"Sorry. No can do. If I come stomping in there, a big US marshal, the sheriff's department is going to think I'm overstepping my boundaries. Besides, Sheriff Ross down in Wendlewood knows you're WITSEC. I'm sure his staff is keeping an eye on you and will smooth things out."

"Really? Because the local deputy isn't aware I'm in witness protection. I'm trying to help her find the killer, but she's still unsure if I'm innocent. Don't you think if she knew I was WITSEC, she'd tell me?"

"I don't know whether she'd tell you or not—different departments do things differently. I suggest you make nice and concoct some sort of excuse about why that ring was in your house."

"An excuse? I can't think of a single reason why that ring would be here. Maybe I should tell them a ghost brought it over!" I hung up on Victor. I missed having a landline, where I could slam the receiver down. Somehow pressing the little phone icon on my cell with force just wasn't the same.

Inside, I flopped down on the sofa before picking up the ring to stare at it. Why was it here?

Allie came creeping out of the bedroom and curled up next to me.

"Bette was here. She sounded freaked out. What's wrong?" Allie asked.

"She lost her ring and is upset about it."

Allie noticed the ring in my hand.

"But it's not that one?"

"No, I'm afraid not. Plus, Victor is being, well, typical Victor!"

"Don't let him take us away," Allie said.

"I won't, honey."

"Because I have a new friend, and that's a good thing, right?"

I hadn't thought about the fact that this ring had belonged to Lucy's grandmother. It had been ripped from her finger either right before or right after her premature demise. I wasn't going to tell Allie, that was certain.

"Don't worry. I'm going to make sure we live here, happily ever after, I promise. Now. Isn't it your bedtime?"

Allie shook her head and crossed her arms.

"Yes. I do believe so." I gently pushed her down the hall as she playfully resisted. Boomer loved our game and barked and spun around us as we laughed down the hall. Laughing was better than crying, and I hoped tomorrow would be a new, less complicated day.

TWENTY

Allie left for school the following morning as I stood on the front porch, watching the way she bound down the stairs to the street, happy to have her newfound freedom. I hoped the kids at school had stopped teasing her about being a baby now that I wasn't escorting her each day.

I screwed up my courage and called Darla Cotton.

"I found some evidence. It's going to make me look bad—really, really bad—but maybe the fact that I'm disclosing it will make it less incriminating."

"Right. I've heard that before. I'm just outside of town, I'll stop by."

"I'll put on some coffee," I said before hanging up.

I bustled around in the kitchen, cleaning things up and making coffee. I left the ring where I'd placed it last night—in the middle of the coffee table. A few minutes later, Darla was at the front door.

"Come on in. Sorry about this, but I really wanted you to hear this from me and not from Bette," I said.

"Bette? What does she have to do with all of this?"

"She was here last night when I found this." I pointed to the wedding ring on the coffee table.

"What is that? Oh, wait. Is that Greta Stramtussle's ring?"

"According to Bette, it is."

"And why is it here?"

"Your guess is as good as mine. I found it between the armchair cushions."

"Strange," she said, tapping the side of her pen against her lips. "I wonder how it got here. I assume you didn't have anything to do with this?"

"I know it looks horrible, but no, I have no idea how that ring could have gotten here." Darla followed me to the kitchen, and I poured her a cup of coffee.

Then we sat on the couch and stared at the ring. I explained how I'd found it in the chair while looking for Bette's car keys, and how Bette herself was missing her ring.

"I can't explain it. My fingerprints are on the ring. I did hold it last night. Sorry. I didn't realize what it was until it was too late."

"There may be some partial prints on it, but it's a pretty small object. I doubt we can get any full images from it—yours or anyone else's. I'd better get my evidence collection kit." Darla trotted down to the street and grabbed her gray plastic toolbox with all the supplies she needed. Using tweezers, she grabbed the ring and tucked it into a plastic bag the size of a business card. She sealed the bag, wrote something indecipherable on the outside of it, and placed it in her kit.

"I don't suppose you have something you want to confess or anything?" Darla asked.

"I confess that I need another cup of coffee, but other than that, I'm as innocent as the day is long." I tried to look as innocent as possible, pasting a beatific smile on my face.

"Come off it. We both know you're not a perfect angel. But

thanks for trying," Darla said, grabbing her kit that contained the evidence as she headed toward the door.

"If I'd truly been guilty, I would've taken this ring and thrown it off a cliff or taken it to Wendlewood and hawked it or—"

"Sorry, it's just you spend so much time doing this job, you start to get suspicious of everyone and everything."

"It's okay. But I assure you. I'm not a bad person. I'm just in transition right now. Allie and I, we've had a rough time, and we just want to settle down in this quaint little town. I want to help you find out who killed Mrs. Stramtussle and Mrs. Heard."

"I wish you'd come clean and tell me what you're hiding, and I sure hope it doesn't have anything to do with these murders."

Before I could respond, she left. I shut the door behind her. Our interaction had confirmed one thing for me—Darla Cotton had no idea Allie and I were in the witness protection program.

It would be another sizzling hot day, so I put on a sleeveless white tank top and black capris. I'd have to put on the horrible polyester jacket and floppy bow tie once I arrived at the hotel for my shift, but in the meantime, this would keep me cool and comfortable.

At the hotel, I once again found myself hauling luggage to the rooms of guests who were checking in. In the lobby, Henry welcomed visitors and gave them pamphlets about the hotel's history and its spooky features, most of which were likely fabricated.

Hauling all the luggage from cars to rooms in my stifling, long-sleeved jacket in this hundred-plus-degree weather was wearing on me. I was overheated and stopped to get a drink in the kitchenette. Searching the cupboards for a mug, I found a gallon-sized black plastic tub labeled *Ectoplasm*. I peeked inside. The container was full of a gooey green substance. It looked like something Allie made once in science class—some sort of slimy concoction made of glue, water, and baking soda. I chugged down a glass of water and took the container out to Henry, just as he'd sent two guests off on their self-guided tour of the property and its resident ghouls.

"What the heck is this?" I asked, shoving the faux ectoplasm at him.

"Keep it down! You want the customers to hear? Put that back—immediately!" Henry hissed, covering the label with his hand.

"What's this all about? What do you do with this, spread it on the door handles, so people think there's a poltergeist?"

He took off for the break room, and I followed. Once there, he grabbed the canister, shoved it in a cupboard, and slammed the door.

"How stupid can you be? I mean, of course there's no real ectoplasm. We have to, how shall I say, provide some enhancements."

"But it's all fake," I said, ready to tear my hair out. "Don't you feel like you're scamming these poor people?"

"People want to believe in ghosts. Why should I burst their bubble? I'm just giving them what they want. And frankly, it's the only way I can get people to come here. Even after all of the promises the Stramtussles made, it didn't happen. I had to get creative."

The Stramtussles. Had they promised Henry ghosts or guests? The paper described Greta as a local real estate maven, so she must've owned this property and others in town. I had to wonder: Could Henry have been angry enough with Greta Stramtussle to have killed her?

And if not him, then how many other people felt she had ripped them off in one way or another in real estate deals? While I had nothing to do with the real estate transaction that landed me in the house on Castlerock Road, I could see why other people might assume that I was just as disgruntled as they were.

Henry and I stood face-to-face in the kitchenette. I said nothing as I looked him straight in the eye, unflinching. I tried to pull myself together and figure out whether I should apologize or bolt for the door. But I didn't have to make that decision. Henry made it for me.

"I think you need to turn in your blazer and bow," Henry said. Without a word, I took off the jacket, ripped off the bow, crumpled them in a ball, and shoved them into his outstretched arms. Then briskly, and with my head held high, I left the hotel.

Once outside, I took a few deep breaths and pulled myself together. I'd lasted at this job for two days. If I looked on the bright side, that was twice as long as I'd spent at the Ferrell's Feed and Tack. I was out of a job once again, and the prospects for employment were few and far between. Why hadn't I kept my big mouth shut? Because I didn't like it when things weren't what they seemed to be. That was the biggest problem I had with my new identity. I was not what I appeared to be.

And now what? Victor would be furious when I told him I'd lost another job. And there was no need to have Flora babysit Allie if I was available after school, not to mention that without a job, I didn't need a babysitter—both of which were heartbreaking to consider.

One thing this job had given me was some insight into Henry Villanueva. He was a scam artist, pure and simple. The Stramtussles had promised him customers or spirits that never materialized. He'd taken it upon himself to make up for it with his theatrics to give his guests the scare they expected. It seemed to be working. While there was never a No Vacancy sign posted, the Hilltop Hotel had guests each night, at least when I had been there. There were so many businesses in town that were struggling, at least Henry had figured out a way to stay afloat.

I did wonder about him mentioning it was the Stramtussles who'd promised him customers. Was that Greta or the whole

Stramtussle clan? Even with Henry's success, did he still blame one or all of them for the terrible business decision he'd made?

I went in search of the sheriff's substation. It wasn't too hard to find, just past Flora Lane's little alley. I opened the door and found Darla sitting in an office not much bigger than a walk-in closet at a government-issue, gunmetal-gray desk filling out paperwork. She looked up as I entered.

"Hi, I'm sorry things didn't go so well earlier today. I really am trying to be a good citizen. I'm actually here because I think I have some information for you about a potential suspect in the murder of Greta Stramtussle," I said.

"Go on," Darla said, dropping her pen and folding her hands together across the top of her paperwork.

"I was working at the Hilltop Hotel, and I discovered that Henry has been faking all of his guests' spooky encounters."

"And what do you mean 'was working'?"

"He fired me for pointing out that he shouldn't be faking paranormal phenomena just to get customers to book rooms."

"His prerogative," Darla said. Her terseness made me nervous.

I grimaced at that and continued.

"Henry's got tourists coming in to stay at his hotel, but maybe he's struggling financially? If Mrs. Stramtussle sold him the property with the promise of supernatural occurrences that never actually materialized, it might be reason enough for him to kill her."

"Possibly. But I could say the same for most of the town—we all have had transactions with Mrs. Stramtussle that were less than satisfactory. Myself included."

Crap. Darla didn't have to say it. I knew she was insinuating that I, too, could fall squarely in that category since I was living in a house owned by Mrs. Stramtussle. Though I had no ax to grind with her, clearly someone did, and I didn't think it was the shrouded, ax-wielding figure I'd seen at her house the night I'd arrived in Paradise.

"Come on, Darla, not everyone in this town can be a suspect."

"True, but you can't come in here pointing fingers at an upstanding community member like Henry Villanueva."

"All I'm saying is if he is dishonest enough to pull off fake hauntings in his hotel, then what other shady actions might he undertake to save his business?"

"I hardly think you can equate some sort of publicity stunt with murder, can you? Especially since what you're really trying to do is distract me from considering the most obvious suspect."

"Really? Who would that be?"

"You."

"I know it doesn't help to say that it really isn't me, but it's not. I didn't know Greta and had no reason to kill her."

"And Mrs. Heard?"

"Okay, point well taken. I did know her, and we had an argument, but nothing so terrible it would be worth killing someone for."

"I don't know about that. I've heard about parents being so uptight about their kid's education, they do some pretty irrational things."

"I'm not one of those parents, believe me." This conversation was not going as expected. "I'd just like to get the murders of these two women cleared up. I have been trying to help you." I wished I could tell her the clock was ticking and that if I didn't get out of hot water soon, Victor was going to yank Allie and me out of town faster than I could say ectoplasm.

Darla was in a difficult situation. I'd helped her by finding clues and pointing her toward various suspects, which had certainly helped her, though she still hadn't apprehended the killer. Admittedly, I hadn't found the clues as much as stumbled upon them, and I had an ulterior motive in the form of guiding her to look at suspects other than myself.

"I'm thankful for what you've done. I wish I could do this by myself, but I can't. You've been able to find things out that I couldn't, and it's been a great help."

That was a pragmatic viewpoint, and I appreciated her honesty. I was certain she hadn't scratched me off her list of suspects, but if I could help her, I was willing if she was.

"Yes. I get it. I know you don't have to believe I'm innocent, but I hope you'll let me help you. So, what's on your mind?"

"First, how are the two victims connected?"

"No idea," I said, shaking my head.

"Me neither," Darla said with a sigh.

"Actually, I do know one way they're linked. They both had a relationship with Meg Stramtussle. Meg works in the school office for Mrs. Heard and was Greta's daughter. At least that's one connection."

"But I don't see how that makes Meg a suspect."

"I talked with Meg and it seems she didn't have a deep and abiding love, or even respect, for either woman."

"Okay, that's good. Really good. Of course I know they're connected but had no idea how she felt about them. How'd you find this out?"

"She just spilled it while we were chatting at her house when I picked up Allie from a playdate. Mrs. Heard aside, I think one motive Meg had for killing her mother was getting a piece of the estate she inherited with her mother out of the way."

"Ohhh. That's harsh, but makes a lot of sense."

"You know all about Meg and Dr. Dan's divorce?" I asked Darla.

"Oh yes! Everyone in town experienced that train wreck. It's all people talked about for weeks—make that months."

"She told me she was struggling financially," I said.

"I didn't know that. Dr. Dan is clearly not paying his child support. I'll see what I can do with that," Darla said, jotting down a few notes on her pad.

"What's next?"

"How did Greta's ring end up in your upholstered chair? Would Bette have hid it there?"

"I don't think she would've planted that ring between the chair cushions while her own ring was missing and while I stood in the room with her—I would have seen her put it there."

"It *is* a pretty small living room, and it would've been hard to miss her shoving something into the cracks of the cushions," she said.

"Though, I did leave her alone while I went to the kitchen to get her a glass of tea, so she could have stowed the ring away then."

"Where'd that armchair come from?" Darla asked

I didn't like where this was headed. It was all too close for comfort to talk about the specifics of my living situation.

"A friend brought it over a couple of days after we arrived."

"Did that friend I met at your house bring it to you? Maybe that's why he looked familiar. I think he bought that chair at our thrift store. Oh, he bought a lamp too."

I actually didn't know who had purchased or delivered my armchair. As far as I was concerned, it had been brought to me by the furniture fairies. I recalled Victor saying he'd picked out some of the furniture himself, so it wasn't completely impossible to believe he'd purchased that chair in Paradise. I decided to play along.

"Yes, he bought it for me. Victor's a good guy," I said, as confidently as possible. I wasn't a good liar, but so far, so good.

"What about him? Maybe he put the ring in the chair."

"Oh, Victor. No, I never left him alone, and he's an upstanding citizen, I promise. Besides, he doesn't have any connection to Mrs. Stramtussle or Paradise for that matter." What I really wanted to do at that moment was tell Darla that he was a US marshal and that there was no way he'd ever plant evidence in the house of one of his witnesses.

"So, if Bette didn't plant the ring in the chair, and neither did Victor, who did?" Darla glanced my way.

"You're looking right at me, and I can assure you it wasn't me. After all, if I'd hidden it, why would I have pulled it out for Bette to see?"

"No idea why you'd do that."

"Gah! It's not me. And it's not Allie. We don't think it's Bette. Or Victor."

"Is that it?" Darla asked.

"You were at my house, but we'll assume you aren't in the business of hiding evidence in citizen's homes."

"Luke was at my house, but he never went inside and was never out of my sight."

"He was? You'll have to tell me more about that sometime," Darla said with a knowing nod.

"Oh, but I forgot to tell you. It couldn't have been Luke who killed Mrs. Stramtussle because he'd driven all the way to Phoenix for a swap meet, and didn't get back until late on Sunday night."

"And he can prove that?" Darla asked.

"I don't see why not. Someone at the swap meet could vouch for him."

"Could someone have broken into your house and put the ring in the chair?" Darla asked.

"That would be a new kind of crime—breaking into a house to leave valuables, rather than stealing them!" I broke out in laughter. I couldn't help myself, it was all just exhausting and ridiculous at this point,

"Do we know about Meg's alibis?" Darla asked, undeterred by my fit of hysteria. "The day Mrs. Heard was killed, I'd gone by the school office to talk with her. She wasn't there—"

"Because she was likely already dead down at the hayride site," I said, finally catching my breath and calming down.

"Right. But Meg wasn't there either," Darla said.

"She told me she'd taken the kids to her ex-husband's house. So, she's probably in the clear."

"Just in case, I think I should look into Meg's financial situation and the Stramtussle estate to see if that could've been a motive for her to kill her mother."

As for me, I promised to continue finding clues as I went about my business, which had become looking for a new job. Again.

TWENTY-ONE

On Monday night, I had an appointment to appear in front of the school board to discuss Allie's grade assignment. I doubted I could convince the board to agree that Allie had been placed incorrectly, even though she had admitted to purposefully failing the test. If matters weren't bad enough, the school board president, Sam Ferrell, was likely still smarting from the injury I'd inflicted on his private parts.

Allie and I had intended to eat dinner at home before walking up to the school, but our plans changed with an aggressive knock on our front door.

"Kelly Jackson, KWW7 TV," the chipper young bleached blond woman said as I answered the door. She held a mic and wore a Pepto-Bismol-pink skirt and blazer with an ivory silk blouse. "I'd like to do a little interview. May I come in?" She barged through the door without waiting for a response, her groggy cameraman trailing behind her. This wasn't good news.

"I, I, don't think—" I stammered.

"I've come to get your comments on the grisly murder that took place right next door. Do you mind?" Kelly snapped her fingers a couple of times to wake up her videographer, who hoisted his camera onto his shoulder.

"Yes, I do mind! You've barged into my living room! I don't want to talk with you. I don't want to be on the evening news! Out! Right now!" I pointed toward the door. The cameraman just stood there, his eyes at half-mast. I snapped my fingers twice in front of his eyes. "Hello? Anybody home? Time to move out!" Apparently, he didn't take directions from anyone but Evening Newscaster Barbie.

"Now, Miss—what did you say your name was?" the woman asked.

"I didn't say, and I'm not going to say. Get out of my house. Now!"

Kelly huffed and turned on her spiked heel, the zombielike cameraman following behind her. I slammed the door as soon as the man cleared the threshold, while Allie looked at me like I'd lost my mind. Maybe, just maybe, I had.

"Why don't you want to talk with her?" Allie asked.

"I don't want to be on television. What if one of the bad guys saw me on the news? He'd know where we are. We wouldn't be safe. For me, it's all about being safe and staying here. That's all that matters."

"You matter most to me, Mom."

"And you to me, baby."

"*Mom.*"

"Sorry, I promise I'll stop calling you that. But you *will* always be my baby, so it's a pretty hard habit to break."

"It's okay," Allie said, giving me a hug. I kissed the top of her head and hugged her back.

"Are you hungry?"

"Can we go out to eat?" Allie asked.

"As long as it's not at Bette's—I don't think she's too happy with me right now."

I got on the computer and looked up restaurants in town.

There weren't many choices. The Hilltop Hotel had a restaurant, but I didn't want to schlep all the way up there. Plus I wasn't sure I'd be welcomed with open arms after being fired. There was a pizza joint up the hill from the school, a little past where we had found Boomer.

I heard a sound on the front steps and peeked out the window.

Kelly and her cameraman still stood in front of the house filming. Lord only knew what she would be saying about how I refused to be interviewed, casting a shadow of guilt across Paradise's newest resident. As far as I knew, Paradise didn't have its own news station. The van had a plastic wrap that read KWW7, and I wondered if that might be Wendlewood's local television station. If they were up here, it must've meant it was a slow news day. Fortunately, the newscaster hadn't gotten my name or any footage of me. I didn't want to come barging out of the front door, and past her, for fear she'd try for one of those guerrilla interviewing techniques, where she trotted along next to me as we tried to make our escape.

"Come on, let's go," I said to Allie, taking her hand and leading her toward the kitchen. "We're going out the sneaky way." We went out the kitchen's back door and down the rickety staircase that put us next to the shed. Then we sneaked around the side of the house and through the yard. We found our way to the street on the far side of the van, out of sight of the news crew.

Allie seemed to like our little adventure, as she walked up ahead of me, leading the way. It made my heart feel good to see my dear, sweet daughter blossoming before my very eyes.

We found the restaurant, Paolo's Pizza. I was relieved it wasn't Poltergeist Pizza or something similarly ghostly; I was sick and tired of fake spookiness. We ordered a large pepperoni pizza with hopes that we'd have leftovers to take home. Allie had root beer and I had a real beer. It felt good to sit and feel normal for once. The pizza arrived. While it wasn't on par with my favorite Italian restaurant in Brooklyn Heights, it was hot and delicious. This place was fast becoming our favorite restaurant in town.

We finished the entire pizza, with no leftovers to take home, and arrived to school at our appointed time, ready to present our case.

I stood ten feet back from the school board members in the middle of the empty basketball court in the school's gym. A metal folding chair had been placed beside me, but I thought standing would be more impactful. Allie sat on the sidelines, in the bottom row of the bleachers. I had instructed her to stay quiet.

Sitting front and center, a smug Sam Ferrell was flanked on one side by Sally Graber, the owner of the clothing store Allie and I had visited on our first day in town. She'd been snippy with me, if not downright unfriendly, that day and also when she'd come to Sam's for supplies. On the other side of Sam was Meg Stramtussle. This seemed a little odd since she was also an employee at the school. I had no idea if there were any rules about conflicts of interest for school district employees to act on the school board. Meg, while she had been polite—perhaps even friendly—to me, did have a reason to look at me with suspicion. First, I was a suspect in the murder of her mother, and second, I'd been accused of the same for her boss.

Sam banged the gavel on the long lunchroom table to bring the meeting to order. This was a pompous move since there was no one else in the room other than the four of us, plus Allie in the bleachers.

"The first and only item on the agenda is Ruby Shaw. She's protesting her daughter's grade assignment after she took our standardized placement test."

It was dead silent. I wasn't sure if it was time for me to speak. No one else said anything. I'd been in situations at least this scary before while discussing my work before panels of art-competition judges, in hopes of winning placement in a prestigious exhibition. Addressing the three people behind the lunch table should have been no different, but there I was, my head buzzing as I drummed up the courage to speak.

Meg Stramtussle, pen poised to take notes, looked up at me. She gave me a little circular gesture with her pen to indicate she was ready, and I should begin.

"Hello and thank you for allowing me to come and speak with you this evening. As I'm sure you're aware, we are new in town, and my daughter, Allie, has had difficulty adjusting. She made a mistake, a big mistake, and purposefully answered questions wrong on the placement test." This elicited a small gasp from Sally Graber. "She's not proud of what she did and has been placed in a lower grade than where she needs to be because of her poor score on the test."

"What do you mean 'needs to be'?" Sally Graber asked, her arms folded, leaning forward in what was either an aggressive posture or a method of adjusting her backside on the uncomfortable metal chair.

"You see, she was in seventh grade before coming to Paradise, and we were hoping that is where she could be—"

"As you know, our school has been awarded high marks for excellence for public schools in Arizona," Sally Graber butted in. "Maybe the school where your daughter was before wasn't so hot."

"She's right," Meg chimed in. "Maybe we just have higher standards."

Meg and Sally were really getting on my nerves. I cursed under my breath—referring to them both using an unflattering term for female dogs. The word echoed off the gymnasium walls amid a simultaneous gasp.

Suddenly, Allie was at my side taking my hand.

"Um, Mom? Don't worry. We'll get the *peaches* on the way

home." Allie made a gallant effort to get me off the hook for my inappropriate comment about Meg and Sally.

I tried to keep my cool. I thought of what Victor had said about flying under the radar. It wasn't going well.

"What did you say?" Sam Ferrell asked, his face turned redder by the minute.

"Nothing, I just—"

"It's okay, Mom." Allie dropped my hand and took a half step forward. "I'm sorry I did what I did. You can leave me in sixth grade. Just know, I wish I hadn't done it. I wanted to leave here, but now I don't as much anymore. I even made a friend."

Meg Stramtussle knew that Allie was referring to her daughter, Lucy. She swallowed hard, set her pen down, and looked at me with half a smile. Meg, who clearly was the junior member of the board, raised her hand tentatively like a shy student asking to be called on.

Sam Ferrell grunted an acknowledgment.

"Maybe we should give Allie the benefit of the doubt. I mean, anyone can do the wrong thing for what seems like for the right reason," Meg said.

Sally and Sam stared down the table at Meg. It was clear from their scowls they disagreed. Allie and I stood together silently. She had retaken my hand.

"Please step outside so the board can confer," Sam said, a disgruntled look on his face.

Outside the gym, I felt like I could finally breathe again.

"That was a courageous thing you did," I said.

"Someone had to save the situation. You're weren't really handling it so well, Mom. Sorry. Like you used to tell me, you should never call anyone a bad name."

"At least not when they might overhear you," I said with a smile. My daughter could teach me a thing or two about playing well with others. "I hope your speech does the trick."

"Me too because if we're going to stay, I'd rather be in

seventh grade."

I hugged my daughter. I wanted to stay too, but as long as accusations swirled around me, staying in Paradise would be difficult. The more I became entangled in the murders of Mrs. Stramtussle and Mrs. Heard, the more likely Victor would decide it was time for us to leave. If we wanted to stay, I had to find out who killed those women. Once the murderer—or murderers—were found, no one would be suspicious of me anymore. Of course, I'd probably never be on the right side of Sam Ferrell—once you kick a man in the balls, it's hard for him to forgive you.

Moments later, Meg Stramtussle poked her head out the door.

"You may come back in," she said, her expression didn't give us any clue of the verdict.

Allie and I returned to the center of the gym. We gripped each other's hands, standing together.

The women on either side of Sam glared at him, as he sat at the table between them with a disgruntled sneer on his face.

"It's the decision of the school board that your daughter can be assigned to the seventh grade on a provisional basis." Sam slammed down his gavel. Again, a completely unnecessary move. From the scowl on this face, it was clear that Sam had been outvoted two-to-one. Thank goodness Meg and Sally had my back—and Allie's.

As Allie and I triumphantly passed the table where the school board sat, Sam thrust an envelope at me. I was sure that giving me my paycheck just added insult to injury for him.

"Should we go buy some peaches?" Allie asked with a sly smirk once we were outside.

"You knew what I meant. Thanks for saving my a—"

"Mom! Cut it out!" Allie elbowed me playfully in the ribs as we walked home, feeling, finally, like we had turned the corner and found some success in this little town.

TWENTY-TWO

I walked up the steps to our house. Allie trailed behind me, having stopped to tie her shoe. As I reached the front door, I noticed it was ajar. I felt a quiver in my stomach. Had I forgotten to close the door when I left? No, that couldn't be it. I had slammed the door on the newscaster and we'd snuck out the back, so it was definitely shut when we'd left.

Taking a shaky breath, I pushed the door open. Claudia sat on the couch in my living room, as if she owned the place. Seeing her again took my breath away as all the painful memories rushed back. My eyes locked with hers but I remained silent, unsure of what to say or do. Allie hadn't caught up with me, but I heard her coming up the steps.

"Claudia! What are you doing here?"

"I needed to see you," she said.

"Why? What's wrong?"

"I'm worried about you and Allie."

"We're fine. We're settling in. Listen, you aren't supposed to be here. It's against the rules." My throat tightened as I spoke.

"Don't you want to hear about my new place?"

"No, I don't. I really don't." Allie approached, and I pulled the door half-shut behind me, hoping that Claudia wouldn't see Allie on the porch. "Victor already broke the rules by bringing you here once. Don't ruin this for us. I want to make this my home. Allie is doing so well. I don't want her to *leave*." I emphasized the word leave, hoping that Allie would get my message: Leave!

"I understand. Too good for your little sister? Your wild-child sister," Claudia said, taking a sip of a beer she'd taken from my fridge.

"No, it's not that at all. Listen to me. I love you. But I have different priorities, now more than ever, and they don't include you."

"But I'm your sister. I love you," Claudia said, giving me a pathetic smile.

"And I love you." I stuck to my place by the door. I wasn't moving until I knew Allie had left.

"Here, come sit with me." Claudia patted the cushion next to her.

Just then, Boomer came zipping down the hall in his usual exuberant way. I reached down and gave him a scratch behind his ears.

"You want to go out, *Marlin?*" I asked, as I stood by the half-open door. I hoped Allie heard me and had gotten my clue: Go find Darla the Marlin. Boomer danced around me and finally bolted out the door.

"What kind of name is Marlin for a dog? Aren't you going to get him?" Claudia asked.

"He likes to … to … roam around by himself. It's pretty safe here, not much traffic."

"Yeah, just like where we grew up. All I wanted was a better life than living on that dinky farm in Clovis."

"I know. I didn't want that either."

"Hooking up with Ricky—that was my way out," Claudia said.

"Too bad he was so involved in whatever that was—the Mexican Mafia." I thought about my options for getting away from my sister. I wasn't sure what she'd do, but it seemed like she was in more trouble than I'd ever understood before. She was desperate and that made her dangerous.

"Ricky said he'd deal with the man who wanted us to sell his drugs. He said that he'd make sure it was all taken care of, and we'd be his alibis," her grip tightened on the beer bottle as she spoke to me.

"When were you going to tell me that I'd have to lie about what Ricky was doing that night?"

"Ricky blew it, really badly." She slammed the bottle down on the coffee table. I jumped back, accidentally slamming the door behind me. "He wasn't supposed to kill him in the room—"

"You knew about this? You planned this?"

"I wanted out, so yeah, I found a way. You and I get to testify against him. It will all be neat and tidy." Claudia rose from the sofa and came toward me, pleading with me to understand that what she had done was necessary.

She had ruined my life all so she could escape a situation that was of her own making.

"Get out!" I shouted as I grabbed her by the wrist and dragged her to the door.

She pulled a gun from her purse and pointed it at me. Her hand was steady, her eyes had lost their warmth.

"Woah. Now, just calm down," I said, backing away from her but finding myself pinned against the front door.

"I'm going to need your help. First, you're going to testify against Ricky, and you're going to make sure it's clear that I'm pure as the driven snow. Got it?"

"Yes. Got it," I said, my voice shaking. I was buying time, trying to figure out how I could get away from my sister.

"And you're going to do me a favor now and then. Maybe

run some errands for me and let me store some not-quite-legal things here occasionally."

It was time for me to play along.

"Sure, I'll do anything you want, just as long as Allie and I can stay here."

"Good girl. I've got some stuff I want you to take care of for me. Where can we hide it?"

"Follow me." I knew just the place where she could stash whatever she had. I headed for the kitchen, and Claudia picked up a black canvas duffel beside the couch. Once I was out the back door, I slowly stepped down each of the rickety stairs, trying to bide my time until help could arrive. Claudia nudged me in the back with the barrel of her gun.

"Keep it moving there, Trish."

When I got to the bottom of the stairs, I turned to face her.

"There is no Patricia Martinez anymore."

"Right, it's Ruby Shaw, now, isn't it? Well, whatever your name is, keep on moving."

Once we were on the back porch, I paused by the potting table, and let her pass, just a few feet from the open shed door.

"You can put whatever you want in there, under a tarp," I said.

"Oh my God, what's all this? Are you starting a little cactus farm? How cute," she said, her voice dripping with sarcasm when she saw all of my succulent cuttings ready to sprout tiny roots in vintage bottles on the railing. Claudia ducked into the shed to hide her duffel and when she emerged, that's when I leaped into action.

The barrel cactus Luke had given me rested in a pot on the table next to me. I picked up the planter and the cactus and chucked them both at my sister. Instinctively, she shielded herself with her hands and dropped her gun. The plant hit her palms and she toppled backward, the cactus spines piercing her skin. Claudia screamed as the pot and the cactus crashed at her feet.

I knew that move wouldn't stop her for long, but I hoped it would slow her down enough to make my escape.

I backed up fast. Claudia screamed epithets as she tried to remove the spines from her hands and negotiate the broken terra-cotta pot at her feet. I dashed through the yard and around the corner, taking the sneaky back way that Allie and I had already used once this evening.

While I'd hated my white Keds when I'd bought them at Kmart, I was thankful for them now. I knew I could run faster than Claudia, who, as usual, sported heels—never a good option for running. I hit the street sprinting, fifty yards up the hill from my house, and kept going. I hadn't yet reached the switchback, but was fast approaching it.

As I rounded the corner, I was relieved to see Darla in her sheriff's uniform, Allie, and Boomer racing down the street toward me. I was running full tilt, glad I'd been hiking up and down these hills. I'd nearly reached them when I heard tires screeching behind me.

I hadn't accounted for Claudia having a car. She careened up the hill at full speed, headed right for me, but she missed the switchback's curve. Her car skidded as she overcorrected and slammed into a retaining wall supporting the road above. Dozens of rocks tumbled from the top of the wall, crashing onto the hood of the vehicle, scattering debris across the street. Claudia tried to drive away, but the car was wedged against the wall. Darla approached the driver's side of the car, gun drawn.

"Get out of the car. Hands where I can see them." Darla cinched a handcuff around one of Claudia's wrists, securing the other end to the stem of the side view mirror. "You just hold on. I'll be back to you shortly." Claudia cussed as she pulled at the cuffs.

Darla used her cell phone to call for backup. Then, to my utter surprise, she slapped a pair of cuffs on me too.

"No wait. Darla, you don't understand. It's her, she's the criminal," I pleaded.

Claudia looked at Darla with such a pathetic expression, her lower lip trembling in phony distress. I had to hand it to her, she really knew how to lay it on thick.

"No, you don't understand. She's the one I was trying to catch. She's been dealing drugs, I can prove it. Just go look in the shed behind her house," Claudia said to Darla. I swear if I wasn't in handcuffs, I would have punched my sister.

Two sheriff SUVs arrived, and Darla walked me toward one of them.

"You head to Flora's until I get this sorted out, okay?" I told Allie. She stood, petrified, in the street. I hated for her to see me in handcuffs, but there was nothing I could do. Allie nodded, as she and Boomer took off. Thank heavens we had Flora in our lives. What would we have done without her?

Turning to Darla, I said, "That's my sister. It's complicated—"

"I think you've said enough. Get in," Darla tucked me into the back of the SUV and slammed the door.

Another deputy unlocked Claudia from her crashed car, and took her to his vehicle. She whimpered as he guided her into the back seat, his hand pressed on the top of her head.

We arrived at the sheriff's department in Wendlewood twenty minutes later. Victor showed up soon after and gave me a nonchalant wave from the other side of the station while I stood at the bars of my cell. He and Darla talked, just out of earshot. I would have given anything to know what they were discussing.

After a few minutes, Darla wordlessly unlocked the cell door and guided me to a small interrogation room where Victor waited. She put me next to Victor and took a seat across from us.

Darla started. "Why the heck did no one tell me you and Allie were in WITSEC?" Her closed fists gripped tightly on the tabletop.

"That's a question you'll have to ask your sheriff," Victor said, his voice calm and steady. "He knew. It was up to him to inform the local law enforcement."

"Had I known, I could have protected you," Darla said. Her brow furrowed, likely thinking about how these last two weeks had been for me. She muttered something about the chief not having faith in her. Had the chief told her about Allie and me, it could have saved us all a lot of pain. "I could have focused on finding the real murder suspect rather than focusing on you." Darla flung her hand toward me. Granted, I could've been in WITSEC *and* the murder suspect, but I decided now wasn't the right time to bring that up.

"I don't have any influence in this jurisdiction, but I'm going to make some calls. Seems to me the chief made some decisions that put our witnesses at risk. I made a bad decision too." Victor was referring to the night he'd bent the rules and brought Claudia to see me.

"Sounds like you two have a few things to talk about. I need to file a report, and I intend to get to the bottom of this," Darla said as she left the room, slamming the door a little harder than was absolutely necessary.

"I shouldn't have brought your sister to your house that night. I put you and your daughter in jeopardy. It was against the rules, and I regret it," Victor said.

"But now Claudia is in custody, so doesn't that mean Allie and I are safe?"

"That's unclear."

"But no one else knows we're here, right?"

"I'm sorry, you can't stay in Paradise. It's over." Victor shook his head.

I'd done all the wrong things, and now we were going to pay

the price. We were going to have to leave the little town we were growing to love. I was heartbroken, and I knew Allie would be too. At least when we moved, we'd still have Victor. No matter how annoying he could be, I'd come to trust and depend on him like family.

"You'll still be our go-to guy, right?"

"I'm afraid not. I got a little too close to you and your sister on this one, bent the rules and nearly got you in deep trouble. I'm sorry about that. I've tendered my resignation."

"What? You're leaving the marshal service? What are you going to do?"

"I'm not sure yet. Maybe I'll start a garden, that seems to have worked for you." Victor stood to go.

"No. I thought you loved your job," I said, following after him.

"I'm afraid I've been doing it just a little too long."

"I'm sorry." I didn't know what else to say.

"You're the last person who needs to apologize. I'm putting a new marshal in touch with you. She's taking over all of my witnesses. Her name is Sarah Palmer. She'll make arrangements to move you and Allie to a new city."

"Victor, no—"

He gave me an awkward hug. "I'll miss you, Ruby Shaw."

TWENTY-THREE

I was left to sit in the empty interrogation room. What was I going to do without Victor? Sure, he could be a pain in the butt, but I'd always felt safe knowing he was watching out for us.

Darla came in and sat down across from me.

"Hey, I'm really sorry," I said.

"You weren't allowed to tell me. It's okay."

"Am I free to go?"

"Yes, I suppose so. You'll need to come in and make an official statement."

"I will. Can I go and say goodbye to my sister?"

"Sure, but make it quick, someone from the marshal service is coming to pick her up in a few minutes."

Claudia was still furious as I approached her cell. She paced behind the bars like a caged animal, stopped for a moment, looked at me, and started to cry.

I had no tears left—just anger.

"I'm so sorry. I should never have drawn you into this mess. I was trying to get out, I swear. I just needed to do one more thing," Claudia said.

"Right. There would always be one more thing after that," I

said, trying my best to keep my anger in check. The lump in my throat made it hard to speak. "I'm going to have to testify against you now."

"I know. I deserve it, whatever happens."

"Allie and I don't want to leave here, but Victor is insisting on it."

"I won't tell anyone where you are. No one. I promise I won't tell. You're my sister, after all."

I wasn't convinced I could trust her. Was it worth risking our lives to stay in Paradise? I wasn't sure. I wished Claudia would do the right thing for once in her life, but I couldn't be sure that she would. We had a community I hoped would protect us, and Darla knew we were in WITSEC at least for the time being. But would they be enough to keep us safe if we decided to stay? If we chose to stay, would we have to leave WITSEC? I had a sinking feeling the answer to that last question was yes.

Claudia and I grasped hands through the bars one last time. It would be the end. I would never see her again. I turned my back and walked away. Like Allie, I wiped away a tear, hoping no one saw me do it.

Darla offered me a ride back to Paradise, and I accepted. We were quiet in the car for a long time. Finally, Darla spoke.

"First, I've got to say, you're an outstanding actor. I had no idea you were in WITSEC. I wish I'd known, it would have made things much easier on all of us, but I get it—it's part of the deal. You've got to take on a new persona."

"Thanks. It's been really hard on me. I wanted to tell you. Victor thought you must've known."

"I'm afraid not. Sheriff Ross has been dropping a lot of balls lately. He's biding his time until he can retire. He hasn't really cared about much of what's been happening on his watch for a while, especially up in little old Paradise."

"Victor said a new marshal will be getting in touch with us, so Allie and I can move. I'm just sick about it. Allie will be crushed when I tell her we have to relocate."

"I know. I don't want you to go either," Darla said warmly, while keeping her eye on the road. "By the way, what the heck did you do to your sister's hands?"

"Um, I threw a barrel cactus at her," I said, shaking my head in disbelief that I'd actually used a plant in self-defense.

"Whew! You are some sort of badass. I hope you'll tell me your real story someday."

"I don't know if that'll happen. The marshal is coming, and then we'll be gone."

Twenty minutes later, Darla pulled up to the curb outside of Flora's shop.

"You want me to wait?"

"No, I think this might take a while, and we can walk home from here. It'll do us good," I said.

"You've got this," Darla said, her hand outstretched in a wave. "Take care."

Allie wasn't the only one who would lose a friend when we moved.

I found Allie with Flora on the back deck, a plate of elaborately decorated cupcakes sat on a table between them.

When Allie saw me, she threw herself at me and squeezed me in a hug harder than she ever had.

"I was worried I'd never see you again," Allie sobbed into my chest. Flora came up behind her and gathered us both up in a hug.

"Shh," I said. "Of course, I was coming back. I'd never leave you." It was all I could do to not break down crying, myself. I took a deep breath and let out a rattling sigh.

"What you need is dessert," Flora said, grabbing me by the elbow and guiding me to a chair next to a plate of cupcakes. "We spent hours making these. Pretty nifty, don't you think? I've always thought cupcakes have healing powers."

I was glad they'd decided to make cupcakes instead of dabbling with explosives. I was sure they'd attempt that another day, if we stayed much longer.

"They do?"

"Yep." Allie picked up the plate and held it out to me. These were the prettiest chocolate cupcakes I'd ever seen. Each one had been piped with different colors of green frosting to make the most realistic succulent designs. They were almost too gorgeous to eat. "Come on. Pick one!"

I chose the one closest to me with a silver-gray rosette on the top. After pulling back the paper baking cup, I took a bite.

"Oh wow! These are delicious!" I took another bite. Bits of frosting squished through my fingers and crumbs hit the ground. Boomer arrived to clean up the mess.

"Oh no, Boomer, come on, let's get you a treat—chocolate's a big no-no for pooches!" Flora traipsed off to the kitchen and Boomer followed.

"You were brilliant to get my hint about going to find Darla. Not everyone would have caught that."

"How could I miss you calling Boomer by the wrong name? I mean, really Mom, *Marlin* is nowhere close to the name Boomer."

"Good job. You guys saved the day." I gave her a high five, smearing chocolate frosting on both of our hands. We giggled as we licked the mess off our fingers.

"What was Aunt Claudia doing here? I thought no one knew where we were."

"Victor brought her over once to say goodbye to me. He shouldn't have done it. But now we ..." I took a deep, calming breath. I had to be strong. "We've got to leave, sweetheart."

"I know," Allie took my hand and squeezed it tight.

"Flora doesn't know our real story, so we should talk about it more when we get home," I croaked, the lump in my throat made it difficult to continue.

It broke my heart to realize we would need to leave Flora without an explanation. She'd never know what happened to us, and we'd never be able to be in touch with her again.

Flora returned a few minutes later with Boomer crunching happily on a cracker.

"Thanks so much for watching after my kiddo," I said, pulling Flora into a hug.

"Don't get all mushy on me. I'm just happy you're both okay. Seems like there are some mighty strange happenings around town," Flora said, giving us an odd smile. If she had any idea what had happened tonight, she wasn't letting on. I was unsure of what, if anything, I could tell Flora, but she wasn't asking questions, so I let it slide.

"You two better skedaddle, it's late," Flora said. "I'll hold onto these cupcakes. If I get peckish I might need a midnight snack. But you come back tomorrow, I promise there'll be some left."

It was a melancholy walk through the town we'd called home for these last couple of weeks. We walked past the Stramtussle Animal Rescue and Thrift Shop and Bette's Place. The cool sage-scented breeze soothed me. Off in the distance, coyotes yipped. Allie and I turned to each other, mouths agape —we'd never get over our excitement of that strange far-off keening. Turning the corner at the switchback, we completed the last leg of the sad journey to our house. Our house, our home—but not for much longer.

Neither of us said much when we arrived home. I found some clean jammies for Allie, and I got into a nightshirt. We snuggled on the couch, wrapped in the colorful throw blankets I'd purchased on one of our first days in town. We watched a silly game show on television until we were both so tired we couldn't keep our eyes open. I helped my dear daughter off to bed, then I crawled into my own, falling asleep before my head even hit the pillow.

TWENTY-FOUR

Once I was up in the morning, still groggy from a fitful night's sleep, I made coffee so strong it could have peeled paint. With Allie still asleep, I took my mug and went down to the backyard. The back porch was a mess from the broken pot and cactus I'd thrown at my sister. I put the chunks of pottery on the potting table, then gingerly scooped my barrel cactus into the canvas bag Luke had put it in when he'd given it to me.

A row of antique bottles with succulent cuttings in them stood in a neat row along the porch rail. I couldn't take them with me, but perhaps Luke would come and get them. But how would I tell him? And what could I say to him about why we had to leave? Leaving Luke was one more loss I'd have to suffer.

But it wasn't just Luke. It was all the rest of the people we'd met in town. Some I had no problem leaving behind—Sam Ferrell and Henry Villanueva came to mind. I was going to miss Bette and her constant questions, and Flora, though Allie would miss her the most. I'd miss Darla. Since she was law enforcement, there might be a way to stay in touch with her. But it would never be the same.

Our new marshal, Sarah Palmer, called while I was in the

yard, which was perfectly fine with me. Allie wouldn't hear the conversation that way.

"Victor Wilson filled me in on your case. Are you ready to go?" Marshal Palmer asked, a smooth efficiency in her voice.

"We can be ready in a few hours," I said, trying my best to set my emotions aside.

We'd done everything to stay under the radar and had failed spectacularly. Our move would set us back to square one—a new town, new school, new neighbors, and new job—a discouraging list of challenges we'd have to tackle once again.

Once Allie was up, it was clear she realized what moving to a new town would mean, and had withdrawn into her shell once again. She was silent when I broke the news to her that the new marshal would arrive soon. I quietly helped her pack her things. I had already finished packing my few belongings. Much of what we'd accumulated we were leaving behind, but not my beautiful handmade quilts. I carefully folded and packed them into a handled paper bag. They were the one artful touch I'd added to the house I couldn't part with.

Marshal Sarah Palmer arrived at two o'clock. Her perfectly pressed black pants and crisp white shirt spoke volumes. She nodded hello to each of us as she removed her sunglasses and stepped inside.

"Ready to go?" she asked, with calm, emotionless professionalism. She didn't engage in much small talk as we loaded our luggage into her nondescript white car waiting at the curb. Boomer jumped in the back seat with Allie. We weren't going to leave him behind. We'd just have to find a new home that allowed dogs, and we'd need a place that would allow me to continue gardening. I stashed the canvas bag with the small barrel cactus in it next to my duffel bag.

Sarah started to pull a U-turn in the street, heading down the hill toward Wendlewood.

"Mom, can we stop at Flora's for a minute?" Allie asked.

"It's up to Marshal Palmer. Is that okay?"

"Sure," she said as she kept eyes on the road, not even asking us why Allie wanted to do that. I missed Victor. He would have made some sort of wisecrack right about now. I couldn't expect that from this new marshal.

We gave her directions to Flora's.

When our car pulled up to the curb, Allie jumped out and sprinted into the shop. Coming out moments later, Allie held Flora by the hand.

"Can we bring her with us?" Allie asked.

"You two are leaving?" Flora looked from me to Allie, a puzzled expression on her face. "I can't come with you. This is my home right here. It's not about the roof over my head. It's about where my heart is. Where my friends are. Where I can be my best self."

Flora's words rang true. She knew where she belonged. She knew what made her happy. I wanted the same things for Allie and me.

"Excuse us for a moment, Flora," I said to her from the open passenger side window. "Allie, sweetheart, can you get back in the car?"

Allie scrambled into the back seat. I turned to Sarah Palmer. "Can you please take us home? Allie and I need more time to think about our decision."

Sarah nodded. She'd clearly seen this play out before.

"Sorry to bother you," I shouted to Flora. She waved at us, her face slack, as the marshal's car pulled away from the curb. Minutes later, we were back at our house. Boomer was the first to leap from the car, dancing around us as we got out. He was at least as excited as we were to be back home.

"I'll call you tomorrow for your answer," Sarah said as she helped us unload our bags from the trunk. "Given the circumstances of your case, you will need to leave WITSEC if you decide to stay here."

"I understand," I said, taking Allie's hand and squeezing it.

Marshal Palmer left just as quickly as she'd arrived without much more than a goodbye. I had to admit it, I missed Victor.

* * *

BACK IN OUR HOUSE, Allie and I sat on the sofa, thunderstruck by what had happened. I had a huge decision to make. Should we stay in WITSEC? If we did, the marshals would move us, and perhaps move us again if we couldn't stay out of trouble. We'd likely be safer if we stayed in witness protection, but would we be happier? I had to agree with Flora—we should be where we could be our best selves.

But where could we be our best selves? Where were our friends and our hearts? If we left WITSEC, we could live wherever I wanted. We could choose Paradise as our new hometown.

"Are we going to stay?" Allie asked, looking at me with bright, expectant eyes.

"Maybe. Or, we could go back to New York. You could go back to your old school. I could start painting again," I said, glancing her way. "It would be like it was."

But I liked the new me—the new us. I'd watched Allie blossom in Paradise. Who knew what a move back to our old lives would bring? Ultimately, we both wanted to stay, not just because of who we had become, but because of who we'd found and brought into our lives. Sure, some problems and personalities meant small-town life had its ups and downs, but any place we lived would have its own challenges.

A part of me thought this little town wasn't as safe as it should be. Even with my help, Darla hadn't been able to find out who had killed Mrs. Stramtussle and Mrs. Heard. That, along with feeling that someone was out to frame me for the murders of those two women, made me want to leave.

Would a move still be our best bet—with or without WITSEC?

My thoughts were interrupted by a frantic pounding on the front door.

When I opened my door, I was surprised to find a panting Derek Stramtussle standing outside. He bent over, hands on knees, trying to catch his breath.

"Ruby, you have to help me," he said between pants.

"What's happened?"

"I've got a tour in an hour and a half, and Bette's going to kill me."

"Kill you? Why?"

"Because I forgot she'd made an appointment for us—something to do with our marriage. I'd stay and do the tour with you, but Bette's set us up to meet with some sort of wedding planner. I mean, what is there to plan?" Derek had a lot to learn. I'd never been married, but I knew a wedding didn't just happen without a little bit of attention and planning.

"Ah, I see." I didn't really see, but it seemed like the correct response.

"You don't understand. Bette is so excited about the wedding. I can't miss this appointment. She'd be furious."

"Well, we can't have that, can we?"

"So! You'll do it?"

"What? Do what?"

"Lead the tour, of course."

"Wait, no, I wasn't saying—"

"Ruby, truly, this means the world to me, to both Bette and me. Have you memorized the script?"

"Yes," I said, which was a lie. I'd read through it once.

"Excellent! I knew you wouldn't let me down. Here are the keys to the building," he said, pressing a key ring into my hand. "You'll find a costume in the closet in the office."

"Really, because …"

"You'll be fine. It's just a small family group. I promise I'll pay you extra for this. The tour starts at six."

Bette bustled up behind Derek and barged right past him.

"I found my ring in the coffee maker!" she said waggling her fingers in front of me.

"I'm so glad. I'm really sorry about the other night—"

"Ah, sugar, I'm the one who's sorry. I was all worked up over my missing ring," Bette threw her arms around me in a hug.

"About Greta's ring—"

"It's all good. I know you didn't have anything to do with Greta's ring. But how did that ring get there? And where's the ring now?"

Bette always had more questions than answers.

She and Derek rushed off, smiling and waving as they got in the car.

I gave them a thumbs-up as they sped off to their appointment.

TWENTY-FIVE

I didn't have much time to prepare for the tour, and I needed a place for Allie to stay since I'd be out quite late. Allie had been begging to have a sleepover at Lucy's, so I called Meg to see if that was an option.

"Of course, we'd love to have her," Meg said when I explained that I needed her help while I covered one of her brother's tours. "I've got an extra sleeping bag, so just bring Allie and her pajamas."

Once we arrived at Meg's, Allie ran off with Lucy. Their excited squeals brought a smile to my face.

"Good luck with the tour tonight," Meg said. "What's up with my brother, why can't he do the tour?"

"He has some sort of wedding planning appointment."

Meg snorted with laughter.

"What? I don't get it."

"I swear, Derek has been over the moon since Bette finally said yes. It really must be true love if she got him to go see a wedding planner!"

"They seem like such an odd couple. Sorry to be so bold."

"Yeah, they're funny. But love is love, right?" Meg held out her right hand to show me her ring.

"Oh! Your mother's ring," I said, taking her hand and admiring the ring closely. "It's lovely. I'm glad you have it."

"Me too," Meg said, a note of sadness in her voice.

"I have my mother's ring too," I said holding up my hand so she could see my ring. "It's made of silver from Mexico, and the stone is a ruby."

"Just like your name. It's beautiful," Meg said with an appreciative nod.

"Thanks," I said, giving her a hug. My ring was a reminder of the strong and loving connection I had with my mother. For Meg, I was certain her feelings were much more complex and conflicted than mine, but I hoped she could find a way to forgive her mother and wear the ring as a reminder of their bond. "Now, I've got to get a move on. I'm going to do a dry run of the tour before I do the real thing if I can swing it."

I walked into town at half-pace, studying the tour script as I went, but I couldn't focus on it. My mind returned to Meg's mother's—now Meg's—ring. Who had placed that ring in the armchair at my house? Had someone broken in just to hide evidence? That seemed a little far-fetched, but I couldn't figure out any other way.

The ring appeared in a place it shouldn't have been. It reminded me of a card trick I'd seen in Times Square called Three Card Monte. It wasn't so much a fun magic trick as it was a money-making scam. The street hustle was all about finding the playing card with the queen on it. The scammer would lay three playing cards facedown, and then swiftly move them around on a table. The innocent bidder would choose the location of the queen and would lose their money every time, always selecting the wrong card. The scammer used sleight of hand to make sure of that.

Was Mrs. Stramtussle's ring like the queen in Three Card Monte?

Once inside the Haunted History Tours building, I turned on all the lights around the bar and front door. It felt oddly creepy, but I recalled it was all just a manufactured vibe—there were no ghosts.

I found the office behind a velvet curtain that separated the elegantly decorated lobby from the back office's practical furnishings. I stumbled around in the dark office until I found a lamp on a desk to turn on. It was an elegant bronze lamp with an etched image of a cat on it and a mica lampshade. This was one half of a matching pair—I had the other one on my bedside table at home.

Darla said two lamps had sold in the days immediately following my arrival. Victor or one of his WITSEC flunkies had purchased one of them for me. Apparently, Derek bought the other one around the same time. I was annoyed that someone had broken up a matching set, but I guessed those sorts of things were more important to me than they were to them. I had less than an hour before the tour participants would arrive, but there was something bothering me about the lamp.

I called Darla.

"Remember the pair of pretty bronze lamps with the cat design at the thrift shop?" I asked when she picked up.

"I do."

"I've got one in my bedroom."

"One of the WITSEC guys bought it for you along with the armchair and some other things. I was there when they bought that stuff, I just didn't know they were from the marshal service at the time."

"Do you know who bought the other lamp?"

"I could check our records. Want to meet me at the shop?" Darla asked.

"I don't have much time, I'm giving a tour at six. You don't have any other plans?"

"Like I have anything to do in this town."

"Woman, we have to find you a boyfriend," I said. "But I think I may claim Luke."

"Oh, lucky, lucky you," she said, hanging up.

* * *

DARLA WAS ALREADY at the store when I arrived. I found her at the computer looking at a spreadsheet.

"So, what did you find out?" I asked, leaning over her shoulder.

"When did you move in?" Darla asked.

"On Sunday, the fourth."

"Right, because it was the first weekend in October when Derek had his scary reenactment tour."

"When Allie and I arrived on Sunday, we had a sofa and beds —oh, and a kitchen table and chairs."

"On Tuesday, I see a sale of an armchair, desk, nightstand, and a lamp," she said, pointing to a line on the spreadsheet. "Those are the things WITSEC bought for you."

"A single lamp. My lamp!"

"Wow, I've never seen anyone get so excited about a lamp," Darla said, raising her eyebrows in surprise.

"Tuesday is the day the furniture fairies brought it," I said distractedly as I pulled up a chair next to Darla.

"'Furniture fairies'?"

"It was the day the furniture arrived. I was excited."

"Gotcha."

"So, the furniture fairies bought me a lamp. Just one. Why?"

"Because we only had the one. We sold its mate the day before," Darla poked a finger at a line of the spreadsheet.

"Who bought that lamp?"

"I don't know. I wasn't volunteering that day. I was looking into the death of Mrs. Stramtussle on Monday."

"Don't you have it in that spreadsheet who bought the lamp?"

"No, we just log that an item sold but not who we sold it to."

"That's okay because I know who bought it—Derek Stramtussle! It's sitting on the desk in the Haunted History Tours office right now."

"Why are you so damn obsessed about the lamp?"

"It's not about the lamp. It's about what else Derek did while he was here at the thrift shop when he bought the lamp," I said. "I think he planted his mother's ring in the armchair while he was here. Buying the lamp gave him a reason for being here." This was Derek's Three Card Monte—look like you're doing one thing while you're actually doing something else.

"Whoever killed Mrs. Stramtussle planted the murder weapon in my backyard to frame me. Right?"

"Seems likely," Darla said.

"So, let's assume the same person also planted Mrs. Stramtussle's ring, in the chair, but not at my house. They put it in the chair while they were here!"

"Why would they do that?"

"To frame me, of course."

"But how would they even know that the chair was going to end up at your house?" Darla asked.

"I'm still working on that," I said, rubbing my temples.

"Sally opened up the thrift shop on Monday morning because I was at Greta's dealing with the aftermath of her murder. She was also watching her store next door. Then there was the person who bought the lamp," Darla said.

"Right, Derek."

"Maybe, Derek. I'd like to remind you that Derek was leading the tour the night his mother was killed, so he couldn't be the culprit."

"Maybe Bette killed Greta—her future mother-in-law. Did you ever check her alibi? She could be scheming with Derek. Once Greta was dead, he'd inherit half of her estate, after all."

"Ruby, I think you're getting ahead of yourself. We still don't know if it was Derek—or even Bette—who bought the lamp. If they weren't in the store then they didn't plant the ring."

"I know, but it's all we've got so far. Did anything else sell that day?"

"Doesn't look like it." Darla scanned the spreadsheet on the screen.

"But there could've been other people in the store who didn't buy anything—any of those people could have put the ring in the chair."

"Right! Only Sally would know who had been here on Monday."

"The only other people who would have had access to the chair would have been whoever was in here on Tuesday morning."

"That was one of Victor's staff, so let's assume it's not one of them, and no one else came in that day until you and Allie showed up with Boomer." Darla said.

She called Sally, but there was no answer.

"We'll just have to try again tomorrow. I've got to go. Wish me luck!" I said, dashing out the door.

I'd run out of time to do a walk-through since I'd spent so much time with Darla at the thrift shop. I practiced the lines of the script in my head as I rushed back to the Haunted History Tours storefront. I found the closet full of costumes just outside the office where I'd discovered the lamp. I pulled out a gray skirt with a bustle and a bodice that matched it.

I went in search of a place to change. The bathroom was hardly large enough to turn around in, let alone put on a long dress with extra layers of fabric and enough padding to make my backside look appropriately large for a turn-of-the-century fashion statement. I retreated to the office to change.

I set the costume down on the desk, careful not to disturb any of the paperwork on top. I took off my shirt but decided I could leave on my shorts and sneakers—no one would see them underneath the skirt. As I reached for the bodice, one of its drawstrings caught on the desk's drawer pull. With a little tug to loosen the string, a stack of papers toppled to the floor along with the bodice. Rats! Tossing the costume aside, I carefully picked up the documents and gently placed them back on the desk.

One of the pages caught my eye. It was a quote for building demolition from Hardy Brothers Demo Crew. I couldn't help myself. I looked at the proposal's job site designation—33, 35, and 37 Castlerock Road. That jerk! Derek was going to tear down my house and the others as well. But not without a fight. Looking at the date, though, I noticed that the quote was six months old. Derek had wanted to destroy those buildings long before his mother decided to rent them out. Her decision to lease them threw a monkey wrench into his plans—whatever they were.

Then I noticed something else. The recipient listed on the quote wasn't only Derek. Henry's name was on it too. They were in it together. I couldn't ponder any longer, the guests would be arriving at any minute.

I smoothed the papers as best I could, threw on my costume, then went out to the lobby to await my guests. I continued studying the script and the map, so I wouldn't look like too much of a fool when I led the tour.

Visualizing, I walked through the journey. We'd start here, right across from Bette's Place. Then we would proceed down-town to see Sally Graber's shop (formerly the post office), the thrift shop (formerly a bank), and Flora's boutique (formerly and currently a blacksmith's workshop among other things).

Along the way, I was to show them the skinny park in the middle of town with the staircase that allowed people to take a shortcut between upper and lower Stewart Street. I was as ready as I'd ever be, and if I forgot what I was supposed to say, I had the script stuffed in the waistband of my skirt.

Just a few minutes after six o'clock, a middle-aged woman with three teenaged boys pulled up to the curb in a minivan. She seemed a little harried.

"Oh my gosh! We almost didn't make it. Those hairpin turns! I wasn't sure if I could make it all the way up here! I'm so glad we did!" The frazzled woman stopped to catch her breath. She nodded to the largest of the three boys sitting in the passenger's seat next to her. "It's Adrian's birthday. This tour is his present. He would have been so disappointed if we'd missed it."

Judging from Adrian's surly expression, I doubted he'd ever been disappointed a day in his life.

I gave the woman directions to where she could park, then she and the boys gathered around outside the Haunted History Tours front door while I locked up.

"Welcome to Paradise's Haunted History Tour. I'm Ruby and I'll be your *ghostess* on tonight's adventure," I said. I wanted to gag at the word *ghostess*, but I really needed this job if I would no longer be getting the US government's support. I smiled and continued. "Our first stop is Sally Graber's shop, Little Treasures. This building was Paradise's first post office. You can still see the postmaster's insignia on the door. If we look in the windows, we can see the original handcrafted sales counter where citizens could post their letters."

It was sad to see Sally's store closed up. Just another shop to shutter due to the sparsity of tourists coming to town. I continued my spiel as we walked along the street.

Arriving at the park at the center of town, we took some time looking at the old mining cart that had been added as a monument. There were a couple of informational plaques that described Paradise's mining heritage next to it.

I couldn't stop thinking about Sally Graber while the family read about the town's copper mining history. She was the key to solving the mystery. She could confirm that Derek bought the lamp. If no one else had been in the thrift shop that day—something Sally could verify—then we could narrow the suspect in the murder of Mrs. Stramtussle down to one person—her own son.

One thing I'd learned from the disastrous experience that landed us in WITSEC was that the best way to do something wrong was to look innocent while you're doing it. That's what Claudia had done with me. She'd set us up to witness Ricky's crime, and she'd made it look like something we'd just stumbled upon.

My best guess was that Derek came into the thrift shop to plant the ring, but he needed an excuse to be there, so he bought a lamp.

I couldn't explain why he—or anyone for that matter—would want to place Greta's ring in an armchair except to frame someone, but who? Derek wouldn't have known the chair would end up at my house, so it couldn't have been me. Was he trying to frame Darla or someone else associated with the thrift shop?

"Ahem!" Adrian's mom stood with pursed lips. I'd been lost in my own thoughts and hadn't realized the family was ready to continue the tour.

The last bit of the journey took us past Flora Lane's shop, and then up through a residential street that ended at the Hilltop Hotel. It was during this time, when there wasn't much to see, that the tourists started asking questions. They were questions I didn't want to answer.

TWENTY-SIX

"My mom said this town is haunted. She promised us some ghosts," Adrian said. I wanted to give his mother some advice: Don't make promises you can keep.

"The funny thing is, Paradise is a ghost town—well, *was* a ghost town. That means that for a while, no one lived here and the place sort of fell apart. Fortunately, there was a woman named Greta Stramtussle who turned the city around. She took care of a problem with feral cats—they had overtaken the city— and once they were gone, people started to move here. It's grown into a nice little town. All of the inhabitants are quite alive; very few of us are ghosts." I tried to sound spooky but I didn't have it in me.

"Ah, that's so sweet. And where does Mrs. Stramtussle live now?" the mom asked.

Oh crap.

"She died just a couple of weeks ago, unfortunately."

"Wait a minute—I read about her. Someone killed her, right?"

"Yes, well, there is an ongoing investigation."

"Ohhhh, maybe we'll see her ghost!" one of the boys,

younger than Adrian, said.

"Perhaps we'll see some ghosts at the Hilltop Hotel. My understanding is that it's haunted." I was disgusted with myself for playing into Henry's scheme, but I didn't know what else to do. I only hoped Henry Villanueva had his faux ghosts in operating order or else we were going to have some disappointed tourists on our hands.

Judging from Henry Villanueva's expression when I walked in the door of his hotel, he clearly hadn't been expecting me.

He scowled—ready to send me away. Only after he saw the four customers trailing behind me did he lighten up, pasting on a cheerful yet creepy grin.

"Welcome, welcome! It's so nice you could make it to our little hotel for the final stop on your tour," Henry said, brushing past me to usher the family into the parlor. "You just wait right here. Gwen will bring your complimentary dessert," Henry said, as Gwen, a young woman who must have replaced me, rushed off to get the desserts. Moments later she returned with a platter.

"Tonight, we're featuring Boo-berry cobbler," Gwen said, placing a dessert plate and fork in front of each guest. Adrian, the birthday boy, seemed less than enthralled.

"Excuse me, Henry, now that you've got the guests, I'm going to say goodbye to them," I said, trying my best to maintain my professional demeanor. "When you've done your tour, can you please send them on their way?"

"Certainly." His terse reply told me he still held a grudge. Henry pulled me toward him and hissed in my ear. "If you have done anything—I mean anything—to question the existence of ghosts in my hotel, then we will have a problem. Do I make myself perfectly clear?"

"Yes, no problem. I've assured them they will see what they came here to see."

"As it should be. Finally, someone knocked some sense into

you," he said, pushing me away.

"What the heck is that supposed to mean?" I asked, too late, as he stalked off.

I returned to the family to say my goodbyes.

"Okay, everyone. Thanks so much for coming out with me tonight. It's been great having you along for the tour of our little town. I'm going to leave you in the very capable hands of Henry Villanueva and his staff." The family members, who were now tucking into their cobbler, exchanged pleasantries with me between bites of dessert. It seemed I hadn't done too terrible of a job tonight.

Once I was outside the hotel, I slid out of the full-length skirt. Ahh. I was glad I had left my shorts and sneakers on under the costume. I loosened up my bodice and slung the skirt over my shoulder. I looked pretty bizarre but was much more comfortable.

As I walked, a little tickle of an idea formed in my head. A small, pesky notion I couldn't let go of. My thoughts returned to the murder of two women in town. Their deaths had to be connected to the houses on Castlerock Road. Why did Derek have a quote on his desk to raze those houses? And why was Henry's name on the proposal too? Henry's association with the demolition project was puzzling because he'd told me the first time we'd met on the sidewalk outside the Castlerock homes that he, like Mrs. Stramtussle, was in favor of keeping the buildings.

I turned around and headed back to the hotel. Once inside, I found Henry at the reception desk. I needed to know why he was teaming up with Derek to tear down those three houses.

"Excuse me, might I have a word with you?"

"Of course. What would you like to tell me?"

"In private."

"I see. I do have guests to take care of."

The family I'd left in the sitting room after the tour seemed to be entertaining themselves quite well.

"It looks as though they don't need anything right now. It'll only take a minute," I said.

"Follow me," Henry said, stepping away from the reception desk. I followed him down the hall toward the not-so-haunted elevator.

"Get in."

"No, I don't think so," I said, stepping back from him. "We can talk right here."

Henry grabbed me by the wrist and yanked me into the elevator.

"Let go of me!" I shouted, pulling my arm out of his grip and reaching toward the open doors to stop them before they closed. But it was too late. The elevator doors slid shut. Henry punched the button marked R for roof.

"I just wanted to ask you about those houses on Castlerock, but you know, that can wait." I reached over to press the alarm button on the operating panel, but Henry slapped my hand away.

"You think you're so smart," he said, leaning toward me menacingly.

Moments later, the doors opened to the widow's walk on the roof. I bolted from the elevator. Anything to get away from Henry. I paced the length of the deck looking for some way to get down. There was no escape route, and the only thing to keep me from falling to my death was a rusty iron railing.

"Did you ever hear the story of the woman who, having been accused of murder, threw herself from the roof of the Hilltop Hotel?"

"No, I don't believe I have," I said as I shifted toward the far corner of the widow's walk as Henry charged me. I jumped out the way, sliding over to the other side of the parapet. "Are you out of your mind? Are you trying to hurt me?"

"No, not exactly. I was hoping to add you to our cast of

ghosts. But first, you've got to be dead."

Henry launched himself at me again. Clearly, he'd never dodged traffic in New York City. Those cabbies will run you down if you're not quick. I was faster than he was and darted back toward the elevator's open doors. My best hope for survival was to get in the elevator, close the doors, and head downstairs—anywhere but the roof!

As I got within two feet of the elevator, its doors slammed shut. I pressed the call button, but it was no use. The elevator was on its way down without me. Gwen was probably showing the guests the haunted elevator trick. Rats!

"I don't really want to get you in trouble, Henry. Okay?" I looked at him from across the platform. He was breathing hard. Obviously, he spent most of his time in his station wagon, driving through Paradise, while I'd been forced to walk. I was thankful for that now. Henry clutched the rail behind him, steadying himself for one final charge at me. "Let's just take a break."

Henry kept puffing, his chest heaving as he spoke. "You don't know what it's like to give up everything," he said, breathless.

"You'd be surprised to hear that I do."

"No, you can't possibly. I've put everything into this place. Derek said, 'Come, out. You'll make some money.' That's what he said." He rubbed a palm across his sweaty face.

I reached behind me and pressed the elevator's call button several more times. I had the sinking feeling the elevator was in spooky show mode, probably zipping from floor to floor with absolutely no one inside. I decided to keep Henry talking because as long as he rambled about his woes, he'd be less interested in attacking me and throwing me over the railing to my death.

"It's got to be hard. You trusted Derek and he let you down," I said.

"You're damn right I trusted him. We were fraternity brothers, after all. We were there for each other. When my life fell apart, Derek helped me make a new start right here in Paradise. Pretty funny calling this dump Paradise. I mean, who do they think they're kidding?"

"What'd your buddy Derek promise you?" I hoped and prayed that the elevator would open while Henry rambled on.

"Not him, his monster of a mother. She said this hotel would be like printing money. The only hotel in this cute little tourist town. Derek said his mom had given him permission to tear down those houses on Castlerock Road." Henry said. He took a few deep breaths to steady himself. "Yeah, that's right, your precious little house. But then she had a change of heart."

"I'm sure Mrs. Stramtussle had a reason. Right?"

"No, no reason at all. Just up and decided one day she didn't want her little town to get any bigger. Did you hear that—*her* little town. Did she have any idea what it might mean to my livelihood or anyone else's for that matter?"

I didn't say a word, just nodded as I looked him in the eye.

Henry seemed so much taller than me. I realized that I'd slid down the metal elevator door until I was nearly crouching as I leaned against it. He lunged at me.

I tried to dodge him, but his arms were open wide. I scrunched my eyes closed, pressing against the elevator doors, ready for impact. There was a clank of metal, and I felt myself falling backward into the open elevator. My heart was pounding as I opened my eyes, ready to press all the buttons that would take me away from the widow's walk. That was, until I looked up to see Darla in her deputy's uniform looking down at me. My head rested on one of her boots as she stood just inside the open elevator.

"I'll take it from here," she said, not missing a beat.

Henry collapsed onto a bench, knowing he was defeated. Darla held out her hand and pulled me up to stand next to her.

"Do you mind telling me what happened here?" Darla

asked me.

"Henry was just about to tell me why he killed Mrs. Stramtussle."

"Go on, tell us," Darla said.

"She ruined everything. I couldn't take it anymore. She had promised we could tear down those three houses. Then she changed her mind without considering how it affected me—or anyone else! To ensure those houses didn't get demolished, she went and leased them ... to you two! What was I supposed to do about it? I couldn't make my mortgage payment on this albatross I had hanging around my neck." His voice crackled with anger. "I tried to talk with her about it, reason with her, tell her I was in financial ruin all because she'd changed her mind about destroying the three houses."

Darla and I stood speechless, listening as Henry confessed what happened the night Mrs. Stramtussle died.

"I met Greta at the middle house on Castlerock Road and told her I wanted to rent it from her so I could make it into a bed-and-breakfast or a little rental cottage. I needed to earn some extra income, somehow. I was desperate. But she said no, she had made up her mind. There was no other way—she had to go. It was meant to look like a robber broke in, killed her, and took her ring. Pretty clever, eh?"

Darla murmured something positive to encourage him to continue.

"The only problem was that Derek had one of his tours that night. When Mrs. Heard showed up for her role as the masked ghoul and saw me, she ruined everything. She never saw Greta, but she knew I'd been at the house. It was only a matter of time before she spilled the beans and told everyone I was there the night Greta died. So, I knew I'd have to find a way to get rid of her too."

Darla slowly, silently, unhooked her handcuffs from her belt. She kept her eyes on Henry as he rambled on.

"With Greta out of the way, I thought Derek would be ready to evict you two from the houses and knock them down. When his mother was still alive, he'd even gone ahead and gotten a quote for us. But once she was gone, he got all wishy-washy on me. Derek didn't want to go against his dearly departed mother's wishes. The poor sap told me he had to honor those leases. Only once you two moved out could we knock down those houses."

"So that's why you decided to frame Ruby," Darla said, moving inch by inch, closer to Henry.

"I put the broken vase in your yard. I figured that would get you out of the picture," Henry said, sneering at me. "You think I'd have left it out in plain sight otherwise? Of course I was trying to incriminate you."

It took every bit of restraint for me to not reach out and slap Henry.

"Now, Darla, I was hoping to expose you as a crooked deputy who planned to keep the valuable ring that went missing from the crime scene. Then we would be rid of you too." Henry pointed a shaky finger at her. "Sally Graber was keeping an eye on the thrift shop on Monday. When Sally wasn't looking, I placed the ring in the chair. I decided I'd buy something, a lamp looked good, so I had a reason to be the shop. I came back the next day, so I could *discover* the ring and blame you—but the chair was gone! How was I supposed to know that ugly chair was going to end up at Ruby's house?"

Darla and I glanced at each other as Henry filled in the blanks in our theories bit by bit.

"So how did Derek end up with the lamp?" I asked.

"Ah, I was such a nice friend to my dear old pal Derek, I gave it to him as a present. Sort of a sympathy gift in honor of his dear mother who had just passed away."

"Did you frame Luke, too?" I asked.

"Without Luke's land, my ultimate plan couldn't be put in

place, so yes, I did. It worked out better than expected, finding the pitchfork in the back of his truck. I was sick of that eyesore —his little grungy farm down on the corner, right as you come toward our quaint town. Once those houses were gone, and Luke was out of the picture, that whole area could be what I envisioned. A beautiful welcome center, museum and gift shop, with Luke's property turned into a nice, new parking lot. I'd have picked up a hefty portion of the tourists' dollars before they even stepped foot in the town of Paradise." Henry's eyes glimmered with the thought of his commercial dreams coming true.

"But you wouldn't stop poking your nose into everything, would you, Ruby? I even hired you, hoping I could keep an eye on you and distract you from snooping around." Henry closed his eyes and tried to regain his composure. "How did you know to come here tonight?" he asked Darla.

"Ruby thought Derek bought the lamp because she saw it in the Haunted History Tours office. So, she thought it was Derek who had planted the ring in the chair," Darla said. "I was worried Ruby was jumping to conclusions, so I went to Sally's house to find out who had been in the store. Whoever had been there on Monday would be on our short list of suspects."

"We knew Sally Graber would have the answer, but she hadn't answered her phone," I said. "Then I had to get ready for the tour and discovered the quote from the demolition crew. That's what I wanted to ask you about," I said.

"I couldn't stop thinking about Sally Graber, so I went to her house and found her in her garden," Darla picked up where I left off. "She told me you were the only customer to come into the thrift shop on Monday. It had to be you who planted the ring. It had to be you who killed Mrs. Stramtussle."

Darla moved swiftly toward Henry and cuffed him before he knew what had happened. Henry dropped his head to his chest, his hands bound. It was over.

EPILOGUE

Two weeks later, Darla and I stood on the balcony at Greta Stramtussle's cottage behind the thrift shop. I understood now why she loved it here. It was the view, the glorious expanse of wildland opening up before us, the red rocks in the distance. Nestled halfway down the valley were the three lonely houses sitting neatly in a row on Castlerock Road.

"Thank you for making this happen for Allie and me," I said, pulling Darla into a hug. "It's hard to believe this place is really ours."

"The animal shelter was part of a nonprofit and that includes this cottage. It's not part of Greta's estate, so no one gets to inherit it. She kept her philanthropic work separate from her commercial real estate."

"Derek can't evict us?" I asked.

"Nope, he'd have to talk to the president of the board."

"And that is …?"

"That would be me." Darla stood next to me as we looked down the slope. She sniffed a little. I knew what was on her mind.

"But what about your house?" I asked.

"You gave up your house, and it made sense to give up mine too. That way, we could get our parking lot."

"You could've lived here, you know. Allie and I would have found another home."

"I did a lot to make your life miserable," Darla said. "I'm sorry about that."

"But you didn't know. The sheriff never told you," I said. "It's not your fault. You were just doing your job."

"Yes, but I can still be upset about it," Darla said, looking up and giving me a sad smile.

"Where are you going to live?" I asked.

"I'm moving back into my folks' house for a while. I hadn't really moved out, so it's no big deal. I'll keep looking. Maybe I'll move to Wendlewood …."

"Don't you dare. We need you here."

"Actually, there's a hotel up at the top of the hill—"

"Ah, yes, I think I know it," I said with a laugh.

"I hear it'll be on the market soon. Greta left me a little money, a thank-you for all the help I've given her over the years volunteering at the thrift shop," Darla said. "I thought maybe I could turn it into a condo complex. I could live in one and rent out the rest."

"Just promise me you won't try any of those fake ghost stunts for the condo residents, okay?"

"I promise, I promise. Hey, I've got to run. We've got a new county sheriff being sworn in today. Old Irv finally decided to retire after he mishandled a recent WITSEC case you may be familiar with."

"You're kidding, right?"

"Nope, not at all. Want to come?"

"No, I think I'll stay here. Luke told me he'd bring us dinner tonight. And the demolition crew will be there soon. It'll break my heart, but somehow it feels like I need to watch those houses get torn down."

"Are you sure? Because you might be interested in this." Darla handed me a fancy white invitation with the county sheriff's department crest at the top of it.

I couldn't believe my eyes. The new sheriff was Victor Wilson!

Even though we weren't in WITSEC any longer, and he wasn't a US marshal, I knew he'd keep us safe, along with Darla. For the first time in a long while, I breathed a deep sigh of relief.

After Darla left, Allie joined me on the balcony as a wrecking ball smashed in the side of what had once been our home. It felt like a gut punch. I wiped away a tear before Allie could see it.

"You and I are made of strong stuff, remember that," she said, hugging me.

She was right. We were, and we had found our home, for good.

Do you want to be the first to know about Ruby and Allie's next adventures? Sign up for Janice Peacock's newsletter: www.janicepeacock.com/newsletter

A NOTE FROM THE AUTHOR

Thank you for reading Aloe and Goodbye. Writing this book has been a challenging and rewarding experience for me, and I hope you love Ruby, Allie, and the little town of Paradise as much as I do. The town is inspired by Jerome, Arizona and Jacksonville, Oregon. While I have only visited Jerome once, it certainly was the inspiration for the hillside town of Paradise. We have a vacation home in Jacksonville, Oregon, and I love spending time in the quaint town and its surrounding natural splendor.

I hope you'll read the future books in the Ruby Shaw Mysteries. I have many more adventures planned for Ruby, Allie, and all the fun characters who inhabit Paradise, Arizona.

Make sure you're the first to know about the next book in the Ruby Shaw Mystery series by signing up for my newsletter.

www.janicepeacock.com/newsletter

If you are looking for another series, check out High Strung, Book One in the Glass Bead Mystery Series.

ABOUT THE AUTHOR

Janice Peacock is a cozy mystery author who specializes in craft and hobby mysteries. She loves to write about artists who find new ways to live their lives and perhaps catch a criminal or two in the process. While working in a glass studio with several colorful and quirky artists, she was inspired to write the Glass Bead Mystery Series. The Ruby Shaw Mysteries, which are set in a small hillside mining town, were inspired by her trips to Jerome, Arizona and Jacksonville, Oregon.

When Janice isn't writing about amateur detectives, she wields a 2,500 degree torch to melt glass and create one-of-kind beads and jewelry. She lives in the San Francisco Bay Area with her husband and an undisclosed number of cats. Visit Janice online at www.janicepeacock.com.

If you enjoyed Aloe and Goodbye, you may also like the humorous Glass Bead Mystery Series. Click here to check out High Strung, Book One.

facebook.com/janpeac

instagram.com/janpeac

Made in the USA
Coppell, TX
29 March 2023

14952761R00128